# Looks May Deceive You

## Shae Flare

NEWMAN SPRINGS PUBLISHING
320 Broad Street
Red Bank, NJ 07701

First originally published by Newman Springs Publishing 2022

ISBN 978-1-63881-966-0 (Paperback)
ISBN 978-1-63881-967-7 (Digital)

Printed in the United States of America

To Mrs. Shelly Coleman
It was her encouragement that made this all possible!

*All it takes is one idea to create a whole new world.*

—Shae Flare

# Introduction

Far from it are the plans of our lives ever written in stone. What once was a solid piece of ground could crumble beneath our feet like the sands of time, sifting away through the hourglass. I was once a care-free creature with dreams and aspirations. I was once naive of the true darkness, hidden deep beneath the murky waters of the world we call our home. We're so deceived by its opaqueness that we believe it to be crystal clear, black-and-white. But in the end, the sides are so tinged with blood no one really knows where they stand anymore.

It was a late Saturday afternoon when I met the love of my life or, rather, unlife. My advice to you is this—when someone you meet asks you out, say yes. No matter what their gender is, how they look, or what their name is, just say yes because they could be the one and only person—or, in my case, people—who will ever care about you. They could be the only one who will stick with you long after all others have abandoned you, when the weight on your shoulders is the heaviest. I was twenty-six years old when I walked into Merciville Bank in hopes of withdrawing a small sum from my rather-large bank account, overflowing courtesy of my uncle. He had passed a year earlier, leaving me all of his worldly possessions. I had never expected it from him, but he had raised me for as long as I could remember. He taught me everything I knew about painting, working with my hands, and carpentry. There were other things that he taught me—things that, over time, I forgot until I needed the knowledge once more. It was a cool evening, just before closing time, when I walked up to the marble counter. I am short for someone my age. Standing at four feet eleven, my head barely cleared the gleaming stone. I stood on my toes and peered up at the tall man on the other side of the counter.

"Ivan Kristaski. Here's my bank card," I said, digging the picture ID out of my wallet along with the bank card.

My height always made people doubt that I was who I said I was, but I couldn't really blame them. I could pass for an adolescent teen girl with my long crimson hair down and my heeled boots that I loved so much.

"All right, Mr. Kristaski, what will you be doing with your account today?" he asked in a polite, deep voice.

He didn't even glance at my ID, seeming to trust me at my word.

"I'd like to make a withdrawal," I murmured, looking into his exotic burgundy eyes.

If his hair had been a little more white than blond, I'd have said he was albino. Regardless, he was one handsome man.

"All right. What amount would you like to withdraw?" he murmured, polite.

He made no comment about my height and didn't even act as if my height was abnormal for a twenty-something-year-old. It caught me a little off guard, and he had to repeat his question before I remembered how to answer.

"Uh, sorry…I'm out of it today. Could I get $450, please?" I murmured gently.

I was a little lost in thought, thinking about the birthday gift I would get for Daniel, my best friend's son. He smiled in response, typing my requested amount into his computer.

"I can see this. I suppose everyone has a day or two like that," he said as he started getting the cash out of his drawer and handing it to me with my bank card and ID, his fingers brushing mine as he passed them to me.

"Thank you," I murmured gently, smiled sweetly, and started to turn away, brushing a lock of hair back from my face.

"Wait…Uh, n-never mind…," he stuttered, biting his lip when I turned back toward him.

He was blushing lightly, and he was so pale it was hard not to notice it.

"What is it? Do I have something on my butt?" I asked, craning my neck to look at my ass, figuring something embarrassing like that would be the cause of such an expression.

"Uh, no—Yes…er, I mean…will you go out with me?" he stuttered out, his blush darkening.

The question startled me, rousting a blush of my own into my cheeks.

"Name the time and place, Mr.…Rose," I said, glancing at his name tag.

I admit it. I was shamelessly flirting with him. I can't say it was an abnormal action for me. I had always been the shameless sort of flirt.

"How about *Et Toi* at 8:00 p.m. on Monday? Do you…like French food?" he asked, seeming exceedingly nervous.

"I love French food actually," I said simply, giving a nonchalant shrug as if my heart wasn't racing with anticipation.

"S-So it's a date?" he asked, rubbing the back of his neck.

I could tell that he wasn't used to asking people out, let alone a short and sassy redhead.

"Yeah, it's a date," I murmured, chuckling and brushing a lock of my hair back from my eyes, the treacherous piece just a bit too short to fit back into the messy crimson braid I had thrown it up into today.

He blushed, scribbling down something on a piece of scrap paper.

"Text me?" he asked, seeming unsure with the way he'd said it, handing me the piece of paper he had written a phone number on.

"Most assuredly," I said, giving him a wink and turning away, walking out with a sexy sway to my hips.

I have never regretted my decision to go on that date. And no, it wasn't because *Et Toi* had damn good food. It was because I'd found the one person I felt truly safe with even when it came down to the wire and secrets were revealed between us.

# Chapter 1

# Our Secrets

We had been dating for two and a half years when things began to change. Markus had begun to grow distant as though he was trying to push me away. He was no longer the shy, carefree man I had met, acting secretive and treating me as if I were glass. I knew something was wrong and decided to confront him on it instead of waiting for the second shoe to drop. It was on a night we shared a dinner in my beloved family home that I threw my questions at him. He'd been particularly edgy throughout dinner, and it worried me. As I leaned forward and placed the homemade dessert on the table in front of him, I opened my mouth to speak. If we were going to go our separate ways, I wanted us to at least remain friends.

"What is wrong? You've been acting off. It's okay if you want to leave me, Markus. I understand I am just a novelty, not really serious-relationship material," I said gently, hiding my heavy heart and speaking around the pain in my chest.

I was used to it, I supposed. Everyone wanted a go at the tiny redhead. Rarely did I ever have a reason to not entertain such games until I'd met him. I had thought my games were done with, that I could settle down, but I suppose it wasn't something for me in the end. His eyes widened, and he looked hurt, catching my wrist as I began to draw away to my seat at the other end of the table. I froze under his grasp, his expression almost becoming my undoing as I gazed at him, swallowing the pain in my chest.

"I-I love you, Ivan…It's not that I want to leave you. It's complicated…," he said, unable to meet my eyes.

I swallowed down the knot in my throat, biting back the tears I wanted to shed as more and more awful could-bes filled my mind.

"You love someone else. That's okay. I understand. I just want you to be happy."

Oh, how it hurt to say that. He looked as if I'd stabbed him with my words, his pain seeming to echo around me, mixing with my own like a toxic cocktail.

"No, no, that is not it…You're my only love," he said.

I pulled my wrist free and sat back in my chair, leaning back and rubbing my forehead to try and hide my agony at secrets and lack of straightforwardness. The next assumption spilled from my lips without a thought, trying so hard to pry the truth from him.

"You're married…I guess I should've known. You're far too good looking to not be," I said with a heavy sigh.

He was just suddenly looming over me, a flash of movement my eyes couldn't quite follow and my brain couldn't seem to comprehend. He pressed my shoulders into the back of the chair with his strong hands, and I had to fight the urge to shiver excitedly, knowing that bruises would form from such a grasp. Oh, how I loved bruises.

"I'm a vampire! I'm a goddamn bloodsucker. I was afraid we'd become this close, *too close*! That you would find me out and become afraid of me, hate me! I was selfish, far too selfish! I wanted to keep you, but I don't want to hurt you! I'm not human, Ivan. I should never have touched you with these same hands that have killed! I should let you go before your heartbeat becomes more of a temptation! But I don't know if I have the strength to let you go now!" he shouted, gripping my shoulders hard roughly, damn near shaking me with every explanation, making my heart race in my chest.

I was both terrified and thrilled by the confession I hadn't imagined in my wildest of dreams.

"Do it. Don't fight it. Just do it," I whispered, reaching up to caress his cheek as I arched up for him, turning my head to the side.

I wasn't quite sure where my reaction had come from, my masochistic streak rearing its ugly head. But I trusted him and wanted

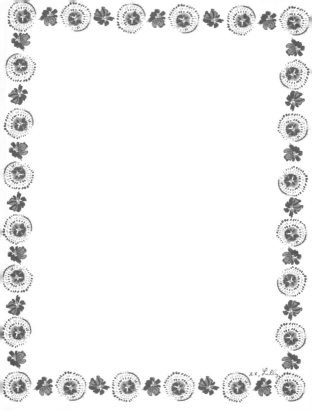

to share everything with him. He pulled away, eyes starstruck and afraid. I caught the collar of his shirt, stopping him, though I knew it was likely I couldn't hold him if he really wanted to get away.

"No, Ivan, no…," he choked out, shocked at my sudden grasp that stopped his cowardly retreat.

"Please, Markus. I'm not afraid! Don't fight it. Bury your fangs in my skin and taste of me, all I have to offer…," I said, trembling and completely unsure why.

He shuddered, his eyes going from flat burgundy to iridescent ruby. His breath came in quick, panicked gasps as he parted his lips, showing fangs that hadn't been there before.

"Oh, God…I want to, Ivan! That's why I can't. I could kill you," he said, trying to pry my fingers free from his shirt; but I held fast.

I may be small in stature, but my hand strength was something I could brag about. So unless he wanted to hurt me, he wasn't getting me to let him go.

"Then I will die happy, knowing I gave you everything you wanted," I said, knowing I wanted this more than anything.

I wanted to give him the blood that pulsed in my veins. I didn't understand it, might never understand why, but I wanted this. I was like a man possessed.

"Please don't torture me like this, Ivy," he all but begged me, eyes pleading.

"I want this, Markus," I said, biting my lip.

I knew he liked it when I acted so soft and sweet, and I knew it was his weakness.

"Not here, Ivy. Not like this…please…," he begged, groaning in protest as he caved to my wiles.

"Then tonight. We'll make it special. Just like when we first made love," I murmured, releasing his shirt.

He drew back and sat in his chair, shakily picking up his fork to poke at the cobbler I'd made. He took a bite of it, awakening a sea of questions that I silenced in favor of my seduction. He looked at me; and I saw fear, love, and concern. He was afraid for me. But I didn't want him to be afraid. I wanted him to be as excited as I felt.

I wanted him to know I loved him and wanted to share all of myself with him.

"I love *you*, Markus. I don't care that you're a vampire. You could have been a unicorn pretending to be human, and I would still have loved you regardless. I'm glad you want my blood. I want to share it with you. I want you to taste me and take what I can offer you," I said, picking up a steak knife off the table.

I spun it on its tip on the table, goring a hole in the wood. I had built it myself, so if I wanted to break it, I would without consequence. I ignored the dessert I'd made. He looked at me, eyes wide, looking so very torn.

"You're the only person I have ever loved. I don't want to lose you to my selfishness, my hunger," he whispered softly, looking so very vulnerable as his eyes slid over my face, reading my expression.

"You won't lose me. Come to bed. I'll light some candles and start a bath. I trust you, Mark. We'll start slow, just like the first time we slept together. You were afraid to hurt me then too because you're so much bigger than me, but you didn't. We fit together, Mark. We just have to start slow," I said, taking his big hand gently, kissing his palm, and nuzzling softly into it.

"All…all right. Slow…We'll start slow…," he agreed softly, eyes heated with the memories of our first night together.

I smiled and stood, turning and heading for the bedroom. I didn't wait for him and went to the nightstand, lighting the candles in the bedroom and the bathroom. I knew he would follow me. I went to the bathroom and had started the bath when Markus slowly inched into the room, expression nervous, the emotion seeming to permeate the air around us. I smiled at him softly and slowly began to unbutton my shirt. I watched his eyes follow my hands. It excited me in an unexplainable way.

"My eyes are up here, sweetie," I purred softly, grinning as he blushed deeply, his eyes slowly sliding back to my face.

"The things you do to me, Ivy. You have me all wrapped up in you, just like the plant you're nicknamed after," he said, moving closer to me, his hands resting on my sides as he looked down at me.

I stood on my tiptoes and kissed his jaw, waiting for him to lean down so I could reach his lips. He did so automatically, and I kissed him soft and passionately, catching his lip between my teeth and tugging softly. He groaned lowly, grasping my hips and lifting me so I could wrap my legs around his waist. I deepened the kiss, stroking his tongue with mine, finding the hard edge of his fangs. But they didn't discourage me. He drew back, slipping my shirt off and kissing along my skin, tongue finding my nipple and circling it slowly. I groaned softly, my breath coming faster. He paused, drawing back. His eyes were iridescent again, the fangs curling over his soft lips, and he trembled as he held me.

"Oh, God...I just want to plunge my fangs into you. I'm so terrible," he cried, tears welling in his eyes.

"Hey, hey, calm down. Slow, remember? Let's get undressed and in the bath," I said, sliding to my feet.

He nodded, swallowing and pulling his T-shirt off. I looked at the familiar scars on his chest and stroked the long, claw-shaped ones.

"Will you tell me the story about how you got this now?" I asked, trying to distract him from his worried thoughts.

He nodded again, sighing softly. I looked into his eyes and could see him slip away into the past.

"Well, I came from a time when our relationship wouldn't have been allowed. I wasn't always gay, ya know," he said gently, unzipping his jeans and slipping them down his hips, revealing a line of golden hair that ran from his belly button down to the small curling ring that encircled his manhood. He'd already sunk into his memories and didn't notice my drooling stare.

"Thank God you changed that," I said softly, prying my eyes from that luscious piece of him.

He was distant as he climbed into the hot water in the tub, disregarding my words.

"I was married to a woman I disliked, and she wasn't like me... She was a monster to me, a wolf, whereas I was a human. We fought often, and she once tried to kill me. That is where I got the scar. I survived. But only because there was a vampire that hated her who was watching us. He turned me into a vampire to torture her. The fact that it saved my life was just a side effect of that torture, not that she actually cared," he said, not much of a storyteller; but it had distracted him as I had hoped it would.

I slid off my slacks and slid into the water in front of him, my back against his finely muscled warm skin. He relaxed some, holding me close and gently.

"I love you, Markus," I murmured softly as he pulled me more up on his chest, kissing the top of my head.

I smiled gently. I was so happy in his arms even as he nuzzled my skin, fangs a hard warning.

"I love you too, Ivy," he said, voice becoming a purr.

He trembled beneath me, and I knew he was desperately clinging to his control as it crumbled from beneath his grasp.

"Do it, Mark. I trust you. Taste what I have to offer you," I urged in a gentle whisper.

He let out a shuddering breath and kissed my pulse, making my heartbeat kick up with excitement and curiosity. Then those warning fangs became a threat as they plunged into my flesh. I cried out, body arching slightly but not in pain. He growled against my skin before he began to drink, holding me tightly. I writhed against him, felt him harden against my thighs, and knew I was just as hard and excited.

"God, Mark! Don't stop!" I cried, trembling as he drank from me, greedily drinking my blood.

I smiled, biting my lip, when he slowly stopped, pulling back. I was disappointed that the moment had ended, but there would be so many more. I lay quietly against his chest when his body beneath me shook as he cried. I turned to face him, resting my face on his chest, kissing his skin.

"Sh, sh, sh. It's okay. You didn't hurt me. I loved it. We're okay," I said, running my hand gently over his soft blond hair and looking into his bloody, teary eyes.

His eyes were even more beautiful this way. I just wish it wasn't fear that made them so.

"You tasted amazing, better than any other, and I didn't want to stop," he said, sobbing softly, small hiccups interrupting his words.

"Markus Rose, you are the love of my life. My blood is yours to have, as is my body. I won't deny you anything," I said, kissing him softly, nuzzling into his cheek.

He kissed back, cuddling me against his broad chest.

"I love you, Ivy," he murmured softly.

I smiled.

"What am I going to do with you?"

"I don't know. But I love you too, Markus. Now let's get out and go to bed," I said, kissing him one more time before getting up and out, grabbing my towel.

I heard him get out behind me and grab his own towel. I turned, surprising him by licking the water from his skin.

"How do you always manage to be perfect?" he asked as he dropped a towel over my head and started drying my hair with gentle hands.

I laughed softly.

"You're the perfect one, Mark. I'm just a pretty face," I said softly, drying his chest and sides with his towel.

"Funny…I've always felt clumsy and embarrassing around you," he murmured, drying my shoulders until I took the towels from him and hung them up.

"Go lie down, big guy. I'll be in in a second," I said, pushing him toward the bedroom.

I sighed as he left and looked at myself in the mirror. My eyes were emerald green, my hair crimson. My features betrayed my Scottish origins, my skin a pale cream that burned if I spent too long beneath the sun. I scarred easily, my eyes sliding over the thin, ragged scar across the middle of my palm, a scar I had gotten when my hand slipped while whittling. I had needed ten stitches, but the bloodstain on the wood had made the little figurine all the more beautiful.

I finished drying off and slipped into the bedroom. There he lay, sprawled out and beautiful on my bed like a gift. I couldn't help the grin that slid across my lips as I looked over his nearly perfect body. I already felt the stirrings of excitement for him, this man, this vampire. He watched me with those beautiful burgundy eyes that I now knew could be an even more beautiful and iridescent red color

17

as I climbed onto the bed beside him. I moved with ease on the slippery silk sheets. He had the comforter draped over his lap and stomach, concealing that wonderful part of him that simply made my mouth water.

"Ivy…you have that look in your eyes again…like you want to eat me," Markus said, a pale, nearly invisible blush darkening his cheeks.

"An accurate analogy," I said as I slowly reached a hand out and grasped the comforter, pulling it off of him and revealing an inch of pale flesh at a time.

Then the song "Paralyzer" by Finger Eleven began to play mutedly, and my audible groan joined it, irritated by the interruption. It was like a wet blanket to smother the mood.

"That's Vanessa's ringtone. She doesn't call unless it's an emergency," Markus said, launching to his feet and getting his phone from the bathroom.

"Your boss?" I asked, an eyebrow quirked at the odd statement.

"My sire's sire's sire. Leader of this district of vampires. She's nearly two thousand years old," he replied before answering the phone and speaking in a language that went right over my head… and not just because I was so short.

While he spoke, I tried to sort out the first part of his explanation. *So she's the sire of the person who sired his sire?* I managed to work out in my head.

But in doing this, I hadn't watched his face; so when he hung up and I focused on him again, I didn't understand how he had gotten so panicked and shaky in a matter of moments.

"Mark…what is it?" I asked, looking at him with a worried expression.

"Hunters…teamed up with the werewolves…and declared war. They've declared war on us…" He gasped out as if in disbelief, putting his arms around me and dragging me close. His eyes were filled with fear once more. "You're not going anywhere out of my sight until this war is finished," he said, lying down with me in his arms and holding me protectively.

So much for sex. That option went out the window as fast as I had when the pastor caught me with his son, and off to sleep we went.

When the morning came, I had to pry my vampire lover off of me to take a shower for work. He insisted on joining me but not for anything fun. My poor Mark was a serious, worried mess, with his eyes constantly on the one window in the bathroom.

"I'm fine, Mark. I'm not going to die taking a shower," I said as I started to shampoo my lengthy hair, working the soap into the thick crimson locks.

"You don't know that! A Hunter or wolf could come through the window and attack you!" he exclaimed.

I turned to look at him, quirking an eyebrow at the absurdity of the statement.

"Marky…the window is literally four inches wide…and it doesn't even open. Nothing is coming through it," I said, shaking my head softly with a sigh, rinsing the soap from my hair.

He growled lightly at my logic, and I pulled him down to kiss him softly.

"Hey, no distracting me, you little devil." He growled when he realized he was beginning to melt into my attention.

"Mm…but I want you to be distracted, Mr. Protective," I purred, kissing his jaw lightly and nibbling at his skin.

"I can't be…Your life is at risk. I can't guard your body if I'm making love to it," he said, pulling away to absently wash his hair.

"Fine. Let me at least have some fun with yours then," I purred and dropped to my knees while he was still so distracted, slowly leaning in to circle my lips around the head of his cock.

I licked softly as I grasped the base and started to stroke him. He let out a startled moan, hardening for me.

"Oh God, Ivy…," he groaned, eyes widening slowly.

He bit his lip softly; and he melted to my intentions, leaning against the tiles as I worked my lips down him slowly, tasting every bit of his hard flesh. He moaned lowly, his fingers lacing in my wet red locks and pulling tight.

I took this as a sign to keep going as I started to lap my tongue around his cock, loving the taste of my man. Urged by his breathy moans, I gently slid a hand up his thigh, caressing his balls and massaging softly.

"You little devil. Ugh…don't stop! I need more!" he growled as he caved completely, his fingers tightening further in my hair.

The slight pain excited me. I loved when he gave into his lust. His primal behavior made me hungry for his climax. He was my everything, and I wanted to take all he could give. Is that really so selfish?

I began to slowly bob my head, my tongue still lapping around his shaft as I took every inch. The hot, hard length slid between my lips, across my tongue, and penetrated my throat. But I loved it. He began to slowly thrust, the telltale sign that he would soon give me his release.

Suddenly he yanked me off his cock, and I whimpered as I lost its warmth from my lips. But then, I was shoved hard against the tiles; and his lips were on mine, kissing me hard and passionately, demanding. I kissed back without hesitation, groaning as he nipped my lip. Then his tongue slid into my mouth, and I was lost to the feel of his tongue tangling with mine. I moaned into his mouth and soon felt the hard caress of fangs against my lips. I pulled back, pulling his head to my neck, my hard cock rubbing against his, making me moan.

"Oh, fuck! Bite me, Markus!" I cried urgently.

Without a second's hesitation, I felt his fangs plunge into my skin. I screamed in pleasure, spasming against him. He held me against his chest with one arm, and I wrapped my legs around his waist. I shuddered in delight when I felt him reach beneath me and grasp his cock, pressing it to my asshole and rubbing it teasingly. Already lubed by my saliva, he started to push into me. I cried out, feeling him fill me, with his fangs still in my skin drinking deeply of my blood. I moaned softly as he slowly began to thrust inside me, struggling against my tightness.

He drew back from my neck with a gasp, blood dribbling down his chin. I instantly followed it to his lips with my tongue, kissing him hard with the heady copper of my own blood on his lips, my tongue tasting his without any hesitancy. His thrusts got harder, hitting that sweet spot inside me that made me moan loudly, my hips bucking. He suddenly shifted into overdrive, hips slapping against me as he fucked me wildly. I cried out, spasming as I came hard, my seed spilling hotly across my chest from my own bouncing cock. He cried out, grunting as he thrust deep, pinning me to the wall and spasming softly as his seed filled my pleasured body. He panted as he kissed me again, soft this time. He drew back and rested his forehead against mine, a small smile curling those sexy lips.

"I could never get enough of this tight, sweet little body of yours. You're my kryptonite, Ivy," Markus purred softly, panting as the water washed over us, rinsing my come from my skin.

"A better analogy would be that I'm the Poison Ivy to your Batman," I said, laughing at the bat pun.

He blinked in surprise, then chuckled.

"I suppose you're right about that...," he said, smiling and brushing hair from my eyes.

"Do you guys turn into bats and wolves and mist?" I asked curiously and smiled when he laughed heartily.

"No. That is a whole load of batshit," he said with a soft smile, kissing my forehead.

"Hey, can you blame me for asking?" I asked playfully, a soft giggle spilling from my lips.

I knew this was far from done, being protective, but I had won this argument today.

# Chapter 2

# Overprotective Bodyguard

"No, I'm not going to call in to work, Markus. I'm already running late," I said, crossing my arms as he ran a brush through my long drying hair.

We had held each other in the shower until the water ran cold and chased us out. Now, Markus was trying to persuade me to stay home while I stubbornly worked on getting ready. Once I'd dressed, his hands on my shoulders had stilled me and pressed me into the seat by the vanity. With gentle hands, he brushed out the knots he'd put in my hair while he was fucking my face.

"I can't protect you there," he started, braiding my hair with deft, lithe fingers.

I cut him off, wincing when the braid became too tight.

"You can't any day. I may be the sub in this relationship, but that doesn't mean I can't take care of myself. Besides, it's not like I work in a private setting. If someone wants to kill me, they'd want it to be less public. I work in a restaurant, Mark, full of people that would notice if a waiter went missing," I reasoned, handing him a hair tie to finish my braid with.

"You don't even need the money. You still have that vast wealth your uncle left you. *I* have plenty enough for the both of us," he protested as I got up and picked up my eyeliner.

As long as I didn't go overboard, I was allowed to wear makeup to work. So a little eyeliner, a little eye shadow, a little gloss, and I was ready for work.

"It's not about money. It's about not letting myself atrophy. It's living while I'm young. Not everyone is immortal, Markus. I certainly am not. I'm not going to allow myself to become spoiled and cheapened by my wealth. My investments won't always be there if I spend them all," I told him as he tried to stop me from leaving.

"Please...I only want to keep you safe. Call in," he said, pleading with me.

I put my hands on my hips and tapped my foot with impatience.

"No. Oh, and be naked when I get home...I want to spend the night with you the way we were supposed to last night. No arguments," I said, heading out the door to my car.

My red 1970s Chevelle was my baby. I had helped my uncle rebuild it, and it still meant the world to me. Markus watched after me as I drove off. I should've known the bastard would devise a plan to play the bodyguard. I just didn't think it would be so damn embarrassing.

Twenty minutes into my shift, I spotted the bastard sitting in the corner booth with a fake mustache on. I even face-palmed automatically when I spotted him and sent Robin to go wait his table so I wouldn't strangle him. He sat there the whole day, getting drinks and a side here or there that he picked at. Finally, before I clocked out, I went up to him with a raised eyebrow and the tapping of my foot.

"Mr. Rose, would you like a to-go box for the ride home?" I asked, a little bit of a bite to my voice as I looked at him with my arms crossed.

"I'm actually...Mr....um...Tulip," he said quickly.

I rolled my eyes, ripping off his fake mustache. He yelped and crossed his arms too as if it wasn't obvious he would be caught.

"Come on. I'll get you a to-go box, and we're gonna go home. You're lucky I love you. I should be kicking your ass," I said, rolling my eyes and going to get the box.

Upon my return to the table, he was gone. I sighed, packed up his food, and headed home.

"I am definitely gonna kick your—"

My sentence cut off as I came face-to-face with a naked Markus on my bed.

"You told me to be naked. I'm naked. Now come here so I can give you what you're craving," he purred.

Ugh, such a sexy bastard. Silly, overprotective bodyguard.

"Ugh, you're lucky I love you," I said again, turned on by his annoying act.

Dropping my bag, I slipped up onto the bed, unbuttoning my vest slowly and licking my lips. He grinned and dragged me against his chest, kissing me eagerly.

"Mm-hmm…very lucky indeed," he purred against my lips before his tongue slipped between them, our tongues tangling excitedly as I threw off my vest and went for the buttons on my dress shirt.

But his hands were there first, ripping it and popping the buttons in his excitement. His lips trailed to my pulse, sucking hard and leaving a hickey on my soft pale skin. I gasped, moaning excitedly, my hand reaching out and finding his cock. I started stroking him, a moan spilling against my neck. My pants were torn roughly from my hips, literally. I would get him later for ruining my clothes. For now, there was nothing I wanted more than him.

My ripped pants discarded, he drew back to snag up the bottle of lube off the nightstand. We never really had to use it much. My blow jobs beforehand always made him slick enough to slip inside me. It was on the nights when he or I were impatient, wanting to be one as soon as possible, that he would pull out the lube. Slicking up his fingers, he pulled me up on his lap so he could gently slip a finger inside of me, his lips returning to my own and kissing me hard and feverishly. A fang cut my lip, but I stopped him from pulling back, the taste of my blood mingling in our mouths. I didn't care; it just excited me more. I gasped as he suddenly plunged a second finger into me and scissored them. I shuddered, moaning lowly. Then his fingers were gone, and he lifted me up. Before I could think, his cock was spearing into my half-prepared ass, making me cry out excitedly.

It was nights like these that I was reduced to nothing but sounds of pleasure. He was rowdy, hot with lust and need. It wasn't even the bloodlust I had started to recognize in him. It was deep and passionate love that made him seem to need me so much. I pushed him back so he lay beneath me, slowly rising up and dropping back down. His eyes never left my body as I slowly started to ride him, still too tight for anything fast—much to his chagrin. I could feel the tension in his body as he fought not to grab my hips and start thrusting wildly. He leaned in, tonguing one of my nipples and drawing a louder-than-normal gasp from me as he plunged his fangs into my skin. I slowly started to move faster on him, loosening up. Suddenly he flipped us, growling against my skin as he started to thrust harder and faster inside me, sucking hard from my flesh. I moaned again, starting to lose myself to the pleasure. I knew I was drooling but stopped caring as he thrust hard, making me writhe beneath him.

"Fuck! You're so perfect! My little love!" he cried, throwing his head back as he started to tremble.

He was getting close. My own body began to tense up, worsened when his hand wrapped around my cock and started stroking in time with his thrusts. They had become erratic, giving me everything I needed as I came hotly across our bodies. He thrust a few more times before plunging deep and coming hard inside me. I felt my body twitch and spasm in delight, the hot feeling making me feel so close to him.

"G-God…my pretty bodyguard…I love you!" I said, panting softly as he slowly pulled out and lay next to me, his arm pulling me flush against his side.

"I will never leave your side. I'll be watching over you until this all blows over, but I will never leave your side for as long as you live," he promised, kissing me softly and lovingly.

The night came to an end in love and pleasure and delight.

\*\*\*\*\*

My poor bodyguard, I'd worn him out. He was asleep when I awoke the next morning for work. Purposely leaving him sleeping,

I quietly got ready, stopping to shake my head at the ruined clothes strewn about the room. He was so grounded for ripping up one of my uniforms. I sighed and slipped out of the house after leaving him a note. He didn't need to show up. Tsk, I bet he'd show up anyway. But hopefully the note would dissuade him and delay him enough for me not to worry about him loitering in the restaurant all day.

When I got to work, it was quiet. Our breakfast shift was normally pretty busy, but it was eerily quiet this morning. Half the staff wasn't even there. In fact, the town on the way into work was far less bustling. I found it odd, especially with the weather being as nice as it was. What had happened in the time I'd been wrapped up in worrying about Markus and his secrets?

"Ivan, the boss says we're gonna close up early today. If no one shows up by the end of breakfast time, we're gonna close up *with pay*," my coworker and best friend, Miriam, said with a smile.

She was a single mother, so it was a relief to her that it would be with pay. She was always struggling to get by. She would never know it, but I was the one that would "leave a good tip." On weeks I knew she was struggling most, I'd drop a few hundred worth in tips on her tables. I had the funds to do it, so why not help her out? She and her adorable son, Daniel, deserved to have a little extra in life. If I had been a straight single man, I would have swooped her up and took her in. I would protect her and the boy as if he were my own. But maybe in another life. We had grown up together and had tried going out for a while. But I knew from the beginning I was a man for men. She was okay with that. It never damaged our friendship as it was said it would. I was just glad that she was there when I needed a friend, regardless of our differences.

"That's great, honey. Why don't you and Danny come over for dinner tonight? Markus has been a pain lately. It would be great to have company to cool his jets," I asked gently, patting her hand as she reached to roll together a set of silverware.

She looked down at me and smiled gently.

"We'd love to. Daniel has been begging me to see his 'uncles' again. You're like a brother to me, so it makes sense that he considers you and Mark as his uncles," she said, handing me the silverware packet to put the little paper holder on it.

"Good. I'll make the little man's favorite. Speaking of, isn't his birthday next week? He's turning ten now, right?" I asked.

Not that I didn't know, I'd already bought the boy a couple of gifts, as well as put aside some "tips" for his mother to buy him a gift. If she ever knew I gave her the tips, she'd kill me for it. She was a woman who fought for self-sufficiency. I respected that and only helped when I knew she was really struggling.

"Yeah. He's a little disappointed that we can't have a birthday party for him, but he understands. He's such a good boy," she said with a sad expression that killed me a little bit inside.

"He'll have a party. His uncle's house is plenty big enough for a party," I said, smiling brightly when she threw a spoon at me.

Oh, how I wished things had stayed so simple and mundane.

"You're spoiling him," she scolded me.

I laughed softly, shaking my head.

"The boy is only young once, 'Riam. Let him be spoiled a bit. He's a very good boy. If he was a tyrant, then me and him would have a long chat. But he's not. So let me spoil him," I said.

Something pinched in her expression. What it was, I wasn't sure because it was gone as soon as it surfaced.

"All right, I guess you're right. I just don't like you handing us things when we need or want it," she said.

I ruffled her hair despite the fact that she was taller than me.

"You worry too much, sis. Breathe for once. Let me handle it," I promised and hugged her softly.

I knew I was missing or overlooking something, but I couldn't decipher it and wasn't going to push her on it. She would tell me when she was ready or not at all. That was her call, and I respected that.

Soon it was almost noon, and the boss sent us all home. I was the last out as usual. I always made sure things were spic-and-span before heading off. It was early afternoon. I was far from tired, so I would be able to get things done tonight.

*That was, if I didn't get done tonight*, I thought with a giggle as I stepped out the back door.

Thoughts of completing a painting and/or wild sex filled my mind as I locked up the door. Then I felt something strike me in the back of the head, and my vision started to go black—but not before seeing that my attacker wore a stark sheep mask, a good-sized rock clutched in their clawed hand. I think it had blood on it too, but my consciousness left me too fast for me to contemplate on it.

*Markus*

I woke to an empty bed and a note telling me that Ivan had gone out by himself. I cursed to myself, planning to scold him for that when he got home. But he didn't come home when he said he would. When the house phone rang, I expected it to be him, but it was Miriam. She asked me to ask Ivan what time he wanted her and Danny to come over.

"He's not with you?" I asked, my heart dropping into my stomach at the news.

Dammit, Ivan, why couldn't you have just stayed home? Why did you have to be so damn stubborn?

"No. The boss sent us home early because of how dead it was today. Is everything all right?" she asked me, worry in her voice.

Her words alone held a sense of foreboding that only I seemed to sense.

"Yeah. He probably just went to get some groceries since he was freed up," I said, panicking but forcing myself to sound normal for her.

The last thing Ivan would want is for Miriam to get involved in anything dangerous. She was far too sweet for it, stronger in her blissful ignorance.

"All right. Have him call me when he gets home," she said softly, voice still worried.

"I will," I promised and hung up, hoping to all hell I wasn't lying to her.

I called Ivan's cell, catching only voicemail.

"Fuck!" I shouted and raced for the restaurant, not bothering wasting time with the car.

My mind and heart were racing in terror.

*Please, God, don't let him be dead,* I begged whoever could hear it.

But my worst fears were imagined as soon as I stopped outside the back of the restaurant. His car was still in its spot, and there was crimson on the steps—Ivy's blood. He was here, and someone had hurt him. I clenched my fists and roared in anger, launching after the faint blood trail of my beloved.

*Ivan*

As I came to, I winced in pain, my head splitting as I cracked open my eyes, worse than my roughest hangover. There was most assuredly dried blood on my face, so that confirmed my theory on the bloodied rock. I could feel the blood crack and crinkle as the muscles in my face moved. Upon further analysis, my vision struggling to focus, I found myself bound to a chair, my arms pulled through the bars on the back and tied there and my legs tied to the legs. A few seconds more and I realized I was gagged too. Man, I had to have a concussion because my analytical skills aren't normally this slow.

"Wakey-wakey, leech bait," a warped voice called to me.

A figure came around in front of me, pulling up a chair and sitting in it with the back facing me, straddling the seat. I tried to tell him to fuck off, but the gag made it hard. He laughed, sounding like a broken machine, reaching up and yanking the gag down. He was still wearing that stupid mask.

"Fuck you. And what is this? Wolf in sheep's clothing? How unoriginal!" I taunted him, spitting in his face.

He growled, yanking off the mask and tossing it to the side.

"Watch yourself, boy. Or you will face a price that your little leech will never forgive you for." He snarled, standing and backhanding me.

I felt my lip split, tasting my blood as the force of it snapped my head back and to the side.

"He won't come for me. He's not that fucking stupid," I growled and spat at him again, blood mingling with the saliva.

*Please don't be that fucking stupid, Markus,* I thought, hoping he knew that I didn't want him to come to my rescue at the risk of himself.

"Oh, he'll come. But not until after we've had our fun," he said.

I heard shuffling from behind me, something going around my throat and pulling tight, choking me for a moment. Then my hands were cut free, and I lunged at the man in front of me, forgetting that my legs were still tied. All he had to do was step back, leaving me to fall flat on my face.

"Fu-uck me!" I yelped, the fall leaving me with a bloody nose and likely a host of bruises.

The bastard started laughing heartily at my foolish attempt.

"Oh, you're going to be fun...I love when they don't break easily. Undo his legs. The fun has only just begun," he said, watching as I was yanked up and the ropes on my legs were cut.

I heard the snap of something heavy and leather, bringing my attention back to the man before me. He held a cat-o'-nine-tails, each little tendril tipped with a metal bead.

"Oh, fuck me..." I swallowed.

That was gonna fucking hurt.

# Chapter 3

# Fucking Madness

*Ivan*

A scream tore from my throat as the cat-o'-nine was brought down hard against my bare back, my skin splitting under the harsh impact from the metal beads. I hated myself for letting them ring another scream from me, but I wasn't about to let them break me. I lost count how many times I'd been struck, but my vision was wavering. Whether it was from blood loss, my adrenaline wearing out, or the stress, I couldn't tell you.

"That's enough, Rafe. It's time we had some other fun. We'll make it so that leech will never want to take him back."

One of the three men growled. I laughed dryly, mocking them as I continued to press my luck.

"You all are so unoriginal. 'Leech', 'bitch', 'fucking whore.' Pfft, I've heard worse from your mother." I spat, clenching my hands into fists where they were chained over my head, suspending me in the air, my shoulders in constant agony.

I don't know how long I'd been there. It felt as if I had been like this for days, but with my back to the window and my wavering consciousness, I couldn't tell if it had been a few hours or days. I was spun to face the brutes, and a fist slammed into my jaw, making me see stars. It rocked me back, and I yelped. But I used the momentum to rock forward, kicking out hard at my abuser. It sent him flying into the other two with a loud thump. I moved quickly, knowing it wouldn't take them long to recover. Dislocating my wrists, I slipped free of the chains and dropped to my feet, taking no time to stop and get my bearings. I just launched off as soon as my feet hit the ground, slamming through the door and bolting down the first hallway I came to. My pain had temporarily disappeared.

*Thank fuck for adrenaline*, I thought as I cut a corner sharply, just barely reacting fast enough to dodge under the reaching grasp of another one of those wolfish bastards.

My elbow found his groin, and he went down with a howl.

The building was a fucking maze, an endless labyrinth of halls and torture chambers. Finally I came to an outer door, slamming through it and hurting my shoulder, something fierce. I felt sun on my face as I ran for the forest, feeling a moment of triumph, only to be brought to my knees as a stunning, paralyzing electric current passed through my body.

"Fuck it all!" I screamed, realizing it was a damned *shock collar* they'd put around my neck.

I struggled with it, trying to get the damned thing off, but it seemed it had a lock combination on it that made it impossible to remove.

"Need a hand?" came a voice I hadn't yet heard, followed by an amused laugh. "Let's get back now, pet. You're only making this worse on yourself," the being purred, grabbing me by the throat, unperturbed by my struggles.

Purple eyes and soot-black hair was the most identifying feature to this man.

"I will fucking kill you," I said, rage seething in my soul.

*Nobody treats me like this*, I snarled in my mind as I was grabbed up and dragged back into the room I'd woken up in.

The door slammed shut, and I heard a lock click into place this time as I was thrown haphazardly across a metal table that had been pushed into the center of the room while I was gone on my failed escape attempt.

"You want to act like a bitch. Let's treat you like a bitch," one of the few goons that still wore a mask said, slapping me hard across the face before grabbing a hold of the collar and yanking me up.

He kissed me hard, and I struggled to keep my mouth closed, his lips bruising against mine. I was slapped again, and he withdrew. There came a clicking metallic sound from behind me; and I was jerked back sharply by it, choked as it was yanked hard against the front of my throat, gasping out as I whirled around, finding the purple-eyed man holding a leash attached to the collar secured around my throat.

"I may be a bitch, but I'll bite anyone who tries to fuck with me!" I snarled, headbutting him as he tried to steal a kiss.

He growled and slammed me down hard on the table by the back of my neck, forcing a choked yelp from my throat.

"Let's see how long you can hold up the tough act," he purred in my ear, the sound of fabric tearing accompanying his words.

He released me, and more hands came to restrain me. I struggled desperately against the hands, twisting to try to see what was happening as there came the clank of metal throughout the room. The man stood by a furnace that sat in the far corner. It was the cast iron kind that was used to heat a room or boil water. There was a roaring fire in it, and something with a long handle sat heating in the flames.

"All this soft, perfect flesh doesn't deserve to go untouched. What better way than to mar it with a mark that will make you forever mine?" he said with a wicked and malicious grin.

His hand grasped the handle, yanking it from the flames and revealing the glowing red brand on the end. He meant to brand me, and that sent a coil of cold fear through me. My struggles redoubled as he advanced toward me, behind me. My vision went white with agony as the red-hot metal was pressed to my back, just above my left buttock. I screamed then, trying to struggle away from the pain. But more hands came down on me, restraining me once more. The pain was all too much, and my consciousness melted into darkness.

*Markus*

I found my way to what could only be considered a prison from hell itself. It had taken me too long to find it. I feared the worst for my little redhead. Three days, he'd been in their grasp. The windows I passed were giving show to a host of nightmare devices meant for brutal torture, making me all the more afraid for him. As I was searching for a place to break in, I heard Ivan's scream through a cracked window a few feet down from the one I currently stood at, and my heart sank. I crept over to it, keeping low and only raising enough to look into the window. The sight inside made me feel sick.

*Ivy…I'm so sorry*, I thought, gagging with tears in my eyes.

He was pinned to a bloody metal table, a collar around his throat with a leash clasped to it. The leash was pulled tight by the man standing behind him. But he wasn't just standing there. He was thrusting hard into him, making Ivan sob and thrash, begging him to stop, that he'd be good. The strong, wild man I knew had been broken.

"Shut up, fang fucking whore. Take it like you're so good at. Mm…help Adam out now. You're not giving him enough attention," the man behind him barked, yanking the leash.

Ivan yelped, the sound cut off as a man appeared in front of him, thrusting his cock into his throat. Ivan gagged, eyes watering as he tried to fight it. His hair had been cut haphazardly, cropped close to his scalp as if they'd known it would humiliate him. I couldn't watch anymore as I dropped into the brush and threw up, trembling harshly.

*Oh, God, Ivy…I've failed you.*

*Ivan*

I gagged, choking on Adam's cock, my eyes watering as I thrashed harder, feeling him dig his claws into my shoulders to hold me in place, more of my blood spilling down my skin. It was as if it never ended, the story repeating with different characters. I felt more blood trail down my legs as Rafael's roughness tore me up inside, the heavy coppery scent of it tainting the air. My vision swam with spots, and Adam drew back before thrusting into my throat hard again. I choked, trying to breathe and turn off my gag reflex, but I was panicking too much to focus on it.

There was a sudden roar in the room and the sound of bones snapping, then Adam was gone from in front of me from between my lips. My eyes fell on who had attacked him, finding an enraged Markus, who bared fangs and launched at Rafael. The impact threw them both against the locked door and through it. I tried to stand up and get down from the table, but my knees gave out underneath my weight. My eyes blurred as I turned to try to see what was happening. But I'd lost too much blood I was going into shock. Markus stood, surrounded by wolves. I felt my body falling and my vision darkening. I cried out for him as a wolf launched at him, teeth tearing into his stomach. Then the world was gone, and I fell into the darkness once more.

*****

As I came to once more, all I could feel was pain. I felt like I had been beaten, which made sense seeing as *I'd been fucking beaten*. I cracked open my eyes slowly and found myself in a hospital room, the annoying beep of a heart monitor in my ear. Well, I was alive, and that was something. But upon further inspection of the room, I found that I was completely alone. I had expected Markus to be in the room, my hero.

A knock sounded on the door, and a nurse came in, wheeling in a cart that contained a computer and a few medical instruments such as sterile needles and bottles of pills.

"Good morning, Mr. Kristaski. How are you feeling?" the nurse asked, hardly looking at me.

He was focused on whatever the computer had on its screen.

"Like shit…," I said, my voice coming out hoarse and rough from Adam's abuse or the screams that had been torn from me.

I wish I could have ripped the fucker's tic-tac off myself, but alas, I had fainted first.

"Respectively. An anonymous caller let us know of your where-abouts. The paramedics found you brutalized, but it looked as though someone had tried to patch you up before fleeing the scene. The police would like to question you once you are feeling better. For now, you need to focus on getting better."

"Has…anyone contacted my boyfriend?" I asked, trying to fig-ure out how that story made any sense.

In my desperation, I tried to sit up and yelped, my back protest-ing the movement.

"Fuck!" I groaned, resisting the urge to shudder from the strangely numbing sensation where the pain should have been.

I lifted my hands to try to push myself up through the feeling and found my hands shook too much to grip the bed railings.

"Please be still, Mr. Kristaski. You were in critical condition when we found you. You ended up needing approximately 150 stitches at least on your back, and there is severe damage to both of your rotator cuffs. So please refrain from harsh movement. You've been unconscious for a full week. We had no information on who to contact. You had no ID or wallet on you. We identified you by fingerprints. They pinged in the system for a loitering charge, and we had your name," he said, turning to me and injecting something into my IV. "I can take down names and numbers of anyone you'd like me to contact, if you'd like," he added, throwing the needle into the sharps box.

I nodded, giving him Markus's number as well as Miriam's, the two most important people in my life.

Once he had left and I was sure I had been left alone, I forced myself up slowly. I was careful as I moved, not wanting to tear the stitches despite my lack of true pain. The room felt suffocating as if I were drowning in the feelings of all those around me. I managed to push myself up and to the edge of the bed, grasping onto the pole that held my IV bag. I was stopped by the cords for the heart moni-tor and ripped them off in irritation, ignoring the screaming it made when it could no longer sense my heartbeat. I quickly hit the buttons on its surface until it went quiet, and I was able to get to my feet without the pull of cords. My body wobbled, struggling for balance,

36

as I leaned my full weight on the pole and made my way toward the bathroom. I had been in enough hospitals, not just as a patient, to know there was a full-length mirror on the back of the door. I wanted to see the extent of the damage myself. I needed to see…what had become of me.

It was a struggle, but I had made it into the bathroom, having a hard time pulling the wheels on the pole up over the lip in the doorway. But I'd made it and slowly shut the door to gaze into the mirror. I started at the top, looking at the mess of my hair. It had been cut close to my head in ragged chunks, the longest of them no more than an inch or two at most. I grit my teeth as the rage surged up in my heart. My eyes slid down, finding the cuts on my face from where I'd been hit multiple times. They wouldn't have been so bad if one of the goons hadn't been wearing gaudy rings. My lip was still split. Another cut at the corner of my lips and one over my left eye in a slash from one of the bastard's claws. Lucky that he hadn't caught my eye as he had my eyebrow and eyelid.

I lifted the hand that wasn't keeping me balanced, the shaking of it catching my eyes as I reached back to untie the hospital gown, the stiff clinical fabric sliding gown my arms until I let it fall to the floor at my bare feet. I sucked in a shocked breath as my eyes scanned down my body. My eyes found the brands on the front of my body. One sat low on my stomach, right at the edge of my hip but above where my pants line would be. The second sat on my inner thigh, close to my groin. I frowned as my eyes scanned them again. They seemed to be far more healed than they should have been in a week's time.

*Was this what he had meant when he'd said about being "patched up" before the authorities had arrived?* I thought.

I took a deep breath, afraid to turn and look at my back. But I turned, relieved that I really couldn't see much other than the blood-ied bandages that were carefully tapped to my skin. I shuddered, horrified by the ones I could see, the raw flesh held together by thick black stitches. I leaned against the sink, hyperventilating as I fought the panic attack that tried to choke me. I was uncomfortable, my skin feeling tight on my bones like I was filled to the brim with fluid. What was wrong with me? Where was the man I had been?

*2 weeks later*

I was shaken awake by Nurse Rhodes, who was attending to me through the morning shift. She smiles at me while pointing to the tray table that extended over the side of my bed.

"Your lunch is here, as well as a few people who'd like to see you," she said.

Then the door opened; and in popped Miriam, Daniel, and my boss, Martin Sharp. Martin was carrying a pretty bouquet of flowers and a get-well-soon balloon. I smiled at them as they made their way over to the bed.

"Hey, guys. You didn't need to come all the way here to see me again," I said softly, but I knew they'd show up.

*Where the hell was Markus*, I thought.

Miriam seemed to know what I was thinking and started to pat my knee but stopped when I flinched in what she thought was pain, but it was only that irritating numbness that still plagued me in its place.

"Sorry. No one has been able to get a hold of him. Frankly it has us all on edge, what with you getting attacked and all. There have been attacks all over the city, and people were going missing. That's why we weren't busy. People were terrified by the attacks and were advised by the news stations to stay in their homes. I suppose that's the downside to not having a television," Miriam said softly, concern written heavily on her face even as she tried to joke.

"Uncle Ivy, are you gonna be okay? Momma said you had gotten hurt and that's why I wasn't allowed to jump on you," Daniel said, piping up from his mother's side, then holding out a little teddy bear made to look like it was sick. "I bought this for you 'cuz a new stuffy always makes me feel better, so I hope he makes you feel better," the boy said, tucking it into the blankets on the bed next to me.

My heart all but melted, and I leaned over, pulling him up on my lap despite the numbness that radiated through me with the motion.

"Ivan, you're hurt, you shouldn't do that," Miriam scolded me.

But I waved it off as I hugged the boy to my chest. I loved him as if he were my own. I wasn't going to let my injuries prevent me from hugging him.

"Thank you so much, Danny. He's making me feel better already," I told Daniel, who grinned brightly and kissed my cheek though I could still feel his concern.

"I'm glad you feel better, Uncle Ivy. It's great to see you again after so long," he said, but it was obvious that he didn't quite believe me as he cuddled against my chest.

I stroked his curly brunette hair gently and jumped as the formerly clear weather was split by a bolt of lightning and the roar of thunder.

"Talk about a sudden storm," I murmured before leaning in to place a soft kiss on the top of his head. "It's great to see you too, bud. I miss you and your troublemaking at my house. I might have to kidnap you for a couple nights like I used to," I joked, remembering the nights I would babysit him overnight when Miriam was working her second job.

"Yeah!" he shouted, smiling.

I spent the next hour cuddling Danny, who insisted that he needed to feed me my lunch, which I obliged. When a ten-year-old holds a fork to your face and insists you eat, you don't refuse—unless, of course, you fancy said fork in the eye or nose. It would be the last meal I ate until I left the hospital, the last of my hope melting away.

Miriam and Danny left late that night, escorted by a police officer. They were being watched over after the events that had occurred. I knew that, if they were to be attacked as I was, the police officer wouldn't be able to do shit. But only I knew that because of Markus.

*Marky…where are you?* I thought.

I hoped he wasn't hurt or dying, in need of me.

This was all my fault.

*Markus*

God, did it hurt. Those bastards had fought dirty, not that I expected anything different from such untamed beasts.

*Ivan…I hope you know I want to be there for you. But I have to heal first. I'll be of no use to you, wounded as I am*, I thought, saddened that I couldn't be there with him.

I moved a bit, lying beneath the earth as I struggled to heal. The wounds in my gut were deep, nearly having been disemboweled. My only solace was the photo of my beloved in my locket clutched in my fist. He had thought I was silly, buying a locket to hold a physical photo. But a cellphone would die, as would he someday die. The photo was permanent. It would be with me forever, long after he was gone and I was all alone again.

A mole dug through the dirt and landed on my face, making me wince as dirt went in my nose. But I wasn't about to snub said nose at a free meal. Capturing the tiny beast, I gulped down its tinny, metallic blood, wishing it was from my beautiful Ivan. But he was hurt too. I wouldn't let him know I needed it when I saw him, because I knew he would insist, and telling him no was hard. There was something about the tiny redhead that just made you want to give him whatever he wanted. So for now, I would spend these hours, days, or weeks—whatever it took to heal—to think of only him and the future I hoped we would have.

# Chapter 4

# The Precipice

*Ivan*

I was finally able to get up and move around my room after another week of being in bed. I'd had a lot of internal tearing and overall damage. The electric shocks had caused my liver to start to shut down. My name was placed on the donor list because it was likely it would permanently fail, not that I cared anymore. Having found that there was a search for Markus's body, I had just given up. Why live if he was truly gone? Miriam disapproved and fought me on it, but I had signed a DNR and had written up a will. She didn't know it, but she and her son were my sole beneficiaries. She would get my wealth, my house, and all of my belongings because I wasn't going to go home.

I sat in a chair by the window, watching the dreary, sunless day with a blank expression. I ignored the nurse as she came in to collect my untouched dinner. It hadn't been a conscious choice to stop eating; I just hadn't been hungry. I felt a pang in my gut, the only real pain that I felt anymore, and waved the nurse over.

"Can you help me into bed…It's hurting again…," I said.

She nodded, helping me to my feet. I lay down in my hospital bed, closing my eyes and sighing as the ache in my gut reminded me that all of this was far from a dream.

"You should eat...Your body is weak as it is. Lack of food is causing it to die further, to shut down faster. You can't just stop fighting," she said softly, looking concerned.

"What's the point? I'm going to die regardless," I said quietly, looking down.

"If you get your strength up, it might help you recover," she said, trying to sound positive.

But we both knew I wouldn't be getting better. I had already given up, and my liver was dying far too fast for any sort of last attempt. She frowned at me and left to get the doctor.

*Markus*

I was finally healed enough to dig myself out. My body was stiff as I crawled out of the dirt into the rainy outdoors. As I climbed out, the mud was washed from my skin. I would still shower before I went to him. Another couple of hours away wouldn't kill him, would it? Oh, how wrong I was.

Without a second's delay, I darted to my apartment and into the shower. After this was all over, I would move in with him... I would finally propose to him. God knows he'd been hinting at marriage. I loved him so much. I had a lifetime to make this up to him for making him suffer like this. I even had a ring, my mother's ring.

*Ivan*

It happened suddenly, without a warning. Pain ripped through my abdomen, and I screamed, hitting the call button as my heart monitor went wild. Blood dribbled down my face from my nose, and there came a flurry of doctors and nurses before the darkness returned to claim my consciousness. I didn't go into that darkness quietly. I went to death's door screaming my pain and agony, like a wild avenging angel.

*Miriam*

Ivan had been in surgery for the last four hours as they tried to keep him alive. Because his heart didn't stop, they could still push for his survival. They hadn't had to resuscitate him yet. I held Danny on my lap, struggling not to cry.

*Ivan, you can't die without knowing the truth. Please don't leave me as the only one to know that Danny is your son!* I mentally screamed, holding him closer.

"Mommy…is Uncle Ivan going to be okay?" Danny asked me, clinging to me.

We raced to the hospital as soon as we got the call that Ivan's health had declined suddenly and rapidly.

*Markus, where are you? You can't be dead. Ivan needs you!*

*Markus*

The house phone was ringing as I got out of the shower, and I frowned, getting a sense of foreboding as I moved to quickly answer it.

"Hello?" I answered, tense as my heart raced, sensing that something awful had come to pass while I had been away to heal.

"Markus Rose?" a tired and morose male voice questioned, sounding like someone at the end of third shift.

"This…This is…," I said reluctantly.

I swallowed hard, trying not to choke on the knot of fear growing in my throat.

"You are needed at Billings Medical Hospital," the voice continued hesitantly, as if weighing how he should go on.

"Why?" I asked, my heart seizing in my chest.

"Mr. Kristaski is in surgery, and it is not looking good. I could get in trouble for saying this, but he is dying. He was told you were dead and has given up on life. His liver is failing, and he signed a DNR. If he dies on the table…they will not revive him. I had hoped one last call would get through to you. He has always been here for those in need. Now it is him who is in need of you," the voice said, trembling. "Ivan was—is a good man. He helped my family when we were…when we were struggling. I owe him this and so much more. So please…hurry. Maybe all he needs is to hear your voice," the person on the other end of the line said.

The phone fell from my hand, and I was gone, barely stopping to throw on clothes.

*I'm on my way, Ivan. I'm coming, my beloved! Just hold on!*

\*\*\*\*\*

Dying isn't nearly as beautiful as the movies make it seem. Dying is cold and unforgiving. The light at the end of the tunnel is like the eye of the storm. It passes you by if you're not careful. It puts you in the hell of the storm and leaves you there. It was horrible. I could still feel my body; but it was broken, dead, and unmoving. I could hear sobbing every now and then and see glimpses of the doctors, Miriam, and Danny. The light seemed only to torture me. I could feel myself crying, but how could I do that as a spirit, here in this void where there should be nothing? I should feel nothing.

Then my connection to the living world was severed, and a figure appeared, standing away from me in this strange void. He was dressed in white with white hair and white eyes. Maybe he was blind. Everything about him screamed power and home. But what was he doing here? Who was he?

"Hello? Hey! Hello! I'm here too! Where are we?" I called after the man in white.

He turned to face me head-on, opening the cupid's bow lips, and seemed to murmur something. But I couldn't hear it. In a flash, I was gone, standing in a place bathed in more whites; and now golds joined the palette. Before me stood another being with golden hair and blue eyes.

"Hello, Ivan of the Kristaski line, man and empath. I am Gabriel, and I am your guide. Why did you give up, Ivan?" the angel asked me, for it was clear he was an angel, unless the wings and unearthly glow meant he was a giant magic bird.

My uncle had spoken of angelic ancestry entwined in the family tree; but I hadn't truly believed him, at least not until now, with one standing before me as if it were a normal everyday occurrence. But then, most people don't die regularly. You only die once.

"Because the man I loved is dead, and I wish to be reunited with him," I said simply, ready to get flak about being gay.

I'd heard it all, and this was an angel after all. Wasn't it taboo or something? But instead, he pulled me in for a hug. He had to bend down to me and pressed his lips to my ear, whispering as if to tell me the greatest secrets of the world without anyone else hearing. But who else was there in this strange limbo but the two of us?

"But, young Ivan, Markus is not dead. Nor are you, not truly dead yet," Gabriel replied simply, as if such news wasn't a knife to the heart.

I felt as though I'd been punched in the stomach.

"Markus...is alive?" I whispered, pain lancing through my chest.

It was all emotional pain. I couldn't feel anything physical. I could barely feel the angel's hug, and even that was more of an imagining of what it should feel like. This was all a little too *Romeo and Juliet*—esque for my taste.

"Yes. He and your son awaits. Now go...You will need a little help to live, but that is what your vampire is for," he said and suddenly pushed me.

I fell back with a cry, falling through the floor, through the void. Falling, it felt as though I was falling forever. Then suddenly nothing but pain!

*Markus*

I. Was. Too. Late.

I felt a scream well in my chest; and it came out as I dropped beside my love who lay on the gurney, pale as I had ever seen, the emotional agony tearing through me like a runaway hurricane. They'd lost him after the surgery, his body failing as soon as he'd settled into the hospital bed. Danny was a mess, screaming that Uncle

Ivan needed to wake up and play with him. The poor boy didn't understand and only made his mother more and more distraught to the point she dragged him out to the waiting room to cry alone with her howling son.

"Ivan, my love, I'm so sorry. Look at you, my beautiful man. You're so cold. They left you uncovered. I'm sorry, Ivy. L-let me cover you up," I said, crying as I pulled the blanket over him up to his chin. I leaned over his face as I looked down at him. He looked as though he were sleeping, but that wild heart no longer beat in his chest. My tears, bloody tears, dripped on his face, landing at the corner of his mouth. It seemed to roll into the crack there, where his lips were slightly parted.

"I'm sorry, beautiful. I'm just so worked up after seeing you again," I said with a pained smile, wiping at his lips with my thumb.

I started to cry hard as I leaned down to kiss those cold pale lips. My bloody tears fell around me as I kissed him, slipping down our cheeks and between our lips, but I didn't care. He was gone, and I just wanted this one last moment and to know his touch for one last time for an eternity. What I didn't expect was for those lips to move or his heart to stutter for but a moment in his chest. Blood. That was it. The blood could wake him, if only for a bit. I'd seen it done before. I could talk to him just one more time.

I stood up and bit into my thumb, fangs splitting the skin and spilling deep crimson as I pressed it to those parted lips. They moved again, wrapping around my thumb and sucking. I gasped softly as his heart jolted to life in his chest, and he shuddered, sucking in breath. His eyes opened, so green and so bright. They were wholly different but somehow still the same.

"Markus?" he whispers in a soft, sweet voice. "He said you were alive—"

"Yes, Ivy. I-It's me," I said as he sat up slowly. "Wait, he? He who?"

"I was dead…but you…saved me…," he said softly and touched his lips as if my question hadn't quite registered in his head.

Then he looked down at the residual blood on my already-healed thumb.

"Yeah, I gave you a little blood, just enough to wake you up but not enough to turn you over to be…like me," I said, expecting him to be appalled.

"If you had given me more?" he asked me, getting that look he got when he was thinking deeply, plotting.

"You would have turned," I said reluctantly, not trusting the look at all.

He grasped my hand, lifting my bleeding thumb toward his lips. I yanked it back from his grasp.

"No, Ivy, I don't want that for you," I said, my heart clenching in my chest at the pained expression he gave me.

"Marky, please. I died, and I don't want that to happen again. Let me do this. Let me be like you," he said, pleading.

My little love, I couldn't do that here, but I couldn't tell him no.

"Not here, Ivan. I want something like that to be special. Let me get the doctor. He'll check you out and make sure you're healthy. Then we can go home," I said, pulling him against my chest and wiping the blood off of his face.

"All right, I trust that you are not lying to me…," he murmured softly, lying back down as I got back on my knees next to the table, wiping my face.

Ivan smiled and licked his thumb, running it down my cheeks.

"Now you look like you were crying like a human," he said, then closed his eyes and lay still.

I took a deep breath, a habit I had never bothered to break.

"Doctor! Doctor! Come quick! He's…he's alive!" I cried, launching to my feet and screaming out the door.

A surge of doctors and nurses came into the room as Ivan pretended to be gasping awake and confused.

*Ivan*

A team of doctors had me in an exam room, checking my vitals and reflexes. Markus was sitting in the corner, watching worriedly. Finally I was told I could go home but that it was likely my liver would still fail. I told them that I would come in as soon as I had any symptoms of said failure though I knew, if Markus kept his promise, I would never die again. The ride home was quiet as neither Markus nor I spoke, both of us eerily quiet. We were thinking about what was to come next. Markus was in a nervous mood. I could feel his uneasiness pouring off of him.

"Marky…listen. It'll be all right. Once this is done…we no longer have to worry about my weakness or if I'll get kidnapped," I said gently, trying to calm him down.

But they were the wrong words to say.

"You won't be the same. You'll change. Everyone does. You won't want to be my Ivan anymore. Maybe not right away, but you'll become bored of seeing my face over the years, and you will leave. You'll find a new man or even a woman that catches your fancy, and you'll walk away. I don't want to see you lose your humanity. I really don't. You're a beautiful, heartfelt, loving man…I don't want to see that melt away, to see you become a cold, unfeeling vampire that only cares about sex or the next feed. Don't you understand…I love you for you, and I wouldn't change that for the world," he said, his hands holding the steering wheel so tight his knuckles had gone white.

But his words had made me angry.

"Markus Rose, I died today. Died. My liver could still fail. If you think that I'll become like that, then you don't really know me at all. I don't want to die because I love you and want to be with you. But…all you care about is what I'll become. You make it out like I'm this horrible monster deep down inside and that turning me will awaken that. If…that is how you really feel, drop me at home and leave. I will live out the rest of my days knowing I was not enough to you and that you believed I would become so horrible. Just know that, this time, it'll be you who killed me…," I said.

The second the words were out, I knew I should never have said them. The pain on Markus's face was so deep I knew I had broken something between us. Then it was as though he shut everything down.

"Then…so be it. I won't have you become like me. I won't make you a monster. I will save you from that…even if it means never seeing you again. Just know that when you are gone, I will cease to ever be happy again. I love you…but…I have seen far too many couples try this and fail. I never intended to turn you from the start. Once you were gone, you were gone. I planned to never be happy after that. I was doomed from the moment you walked into my life. My pretty little Scotsman with the lovely green eyes was going to be my first and last bit of happiness in centuries," he said, pulling up to my house.

"That was foolish and selfish. You led us both toward pain without caring at all about how I would feel. Goodbye, Markus. Have a great eternity. I never thought…I'd be the last of the Kristaski line. I always hoped I'd have children before I died. But then I found out I was gay, and that doesn't make babies. I'm just the world's greatest screwup. I suppose I fell in love with the wrong gender, the wrong guy, and the wrong species all in one go…," I said, sobbing softly as I turned and darted inside before he could answer.

It was too late for anything else. It was over, and I was going to die again. I should have just died before and saved myself from all the pain.

*Fuck. Death better come quicker this time. I have even less of a reason to live now.*

# Chapter 5

# Simpler Times

In my time alone, I found myself reliving the memories of simpler times—time when all was right in my world and I was happy, when we were happy together. Now that they were gone and all I had were the memories, I savored them as if they were my last lifeline; and in a way, they were.

*One year earlier*
*Ivan*

I lay on my couch, curled up as I watched *The Devil Is a Part-Time*r on Netflix. Anime was my stress reliever. Even after dating Mr. Rose for a month, I still got nervous about dates. Tonight we were just going to have a night inside with Chinese delivery and a *Futurama* marathon. With a sigh, I paused just before Ciel smacked Lucifer in the back of the head, and pushed to my feet. I needed to shower and put on my warm flannel pants and oversized Guns N' Roses T-shirt, a comfortable outfit for a comfortable date. It may or may not have been Markus's. But he thought I was "too cute" to take it back. I trudged into the bathroom and stripped, taking a quick warm shower. Once I was out of the shower, I called the Chinese place while dressed.

"I need an order of Happy Family with chicken fried rice and an order of crab rangoons, then an order of beef lo mein," I said to the nice lady on the phone, pulling up my pants with one hand to keep the phone to my ear. "One extra white rice would be good," I answered, cradling the phone between my shoulder and ear as I tied the drawstring on the pants.

My waist was too petite for most men's pants, especially in pajama bottoms.

"That would be all. All right, thank you," I murmured as she accepted my order and said goodbye.

I hung up and pulled Markus's shirt over my shoulder, breathing in his cologne that somehow still clung to the shirt despite having been washed since he'd worn it. I loved the way he smelled, like a forest after rain but with a tang of civilization. It was amazing. I heard the doorbell ring and felt my heart jerk in my chest. It had to be him; the Chinese delivery wouldn't arrive for another forty-five minutes. I all but ran downstairs and opened the door to my beloved boyfriend, standing just out of the rain at my door.

"Hey, Ivan," he murmured, giving me that heartbreakingly beautiful smile.

I grabbed his hand and pulled him inside.

"Get in here before you catch your death in the cold out there!" I exclaimed as I looked at him in a pair of plush pajama pants and a matching silk button-up pajama top. He looked so cozy and like a luxury pajama model.

"I needn't worry about the cold, Ivan, because my heart was warmed by that smile of yours, and that was all I needed…," he said, trying to be suave and sweet but unable to help his shy insecurity.

I felt myself blush, and I swatted him.

"Oh, shush. Come on. We're starting the show from the beginning since some of us have never seen it before. I'm not mentioning any names," I said but gave him a pointed look as it was he who had never seen the show before.

He laughed and blushed, shaking his head at me as I pulled him onto the couch and plopped down next to him, turning on the show. Episode one of course.

*****

Soon it was almost 10:00 p.m., and I was starting to get some… ideas about what I wanted to do for the rest of the night's sleepover. We lay spooning on the couch, I as the little spoon. Markus's arms tightened around me as I "accidentally" ground my ass against his crotch.

"Ivan…what are you doing?" he asked softly, suspicion in his tone.

"Well, Markus, I want to…have sex with you," I said, blushing as I turned in his arms.

He frowned, looking down at me with a confused expression.

"Ivan…no. I'm too big, and you're so delicate. I don't want to hurt you," he said, holding me closer.

I rolled my eyes.

"Come on…please. We'll go slow, and if anything hurts…I'll say something," I begged, giving him the eyes I knew he couldn't resist.

"I—All right…but…promise me you'll say something as *soon* as it hurts," he all but pleaded with me, and I eagerly nodded.

Then I was pulling him toward my room, a grin curling my lips. Finally he had agreed.

I backed him up until he hit the edge of my bed and playfully pushed him backward across the sheets. He caught my waist as he fell, pulling me down with him. We kissed deeply, his tongue moving smoothly against mine. I nipped his lip before kissing down his jaw to the collar of his pajama top, my hands sliding up the silk and finding the first button. His hands found my hips, and he squeezed me against him as my hands worked to undo the buttons of his shirt. My lips followed the skin that I bared, my tongue darting across one of his nipples when the shirt edge fell away from his chest. He gasped out softly, and I glanced up at his face, delighted by the slight blush on his cheeks and lust-filled eyes.

"Mmph…Ivan…," he panted out, grabbing the hem of the pilfered T-shirt I wore and pulling it quickly over my head.

I kissed him hard again, giggling when I felt his fingers fumble with the knot on my pajama pants.

"I'll get it, big boy. You get yours," I purred in his ear, nipping his earlobe softly before rolling off of him and standing to slip out of my pants.

I bent and slowly pulled them off from around my ankles, smirking when I heard a sharp intake of breath. Looking over my shoulders, I met his eyes and grinned. Turning and climbing back up on the bed, I leaned in for a kiss. When he pulled back suddenly, I frowned softly.

"I'm…I'm too big. I…I don't wanna hurt you…," he stuttered out nervously, blushing deeper than I had ever seen him blush.

My eyes slid down his chest until they fell on what he considered the problem. Golden curls surrounded a delicious length like a crown, and I nearly drooled just looking.

"Mmph…Marky…I'm not worried," I said, inching closer to him. With a hand on his chest, I got him to lie back for me. "But I definitely am gonna need a taste test first," I added, carefully curling my fingers around the base of him.

I felt a little quiver deep in my belly as I felt that warm thickness in my grasp. Without giving him a chance to respond, I leaned down and sucked the tip of him into my mouth. I couldn't help the little groan that slipped from me at the taste of him. I felt him shudder beneath my grasp and, since he didn't protest, slowly took him into my mouth. My tongue worked over every vein and wrinkle of his skin, learning him. This was the man I loved. I wanted to memorize every tasty inch of him.

"I-Ivan…no more. I…I need you." His voice penetrated my delighted thoughts as the heat in my mouth jerked in excitement.

I reluctantly drew up off of him, frowning playfully.

"Aw, but I was having so much fun," I teased, thumbing the tip of his cock lightly.

He groaned softly and shook his head.

"Please...," he pleaded.

I grinned, straddling him carefully and biting my lip as my own hard cock rubbed against his belly.

"All right. But only because you asked oh so nicely," I said, reaching down and grasping him carefully, lining him up with my already-throbbing asshole. "It'll be a bit tight without lube at first, but don't panic," I told him softly before slowly starting to press down onto him.

My breath whooshed from my lungs as the head of his cock popped past the ring of muscle, my teeth burying themselves in my lip as a groan spilled toward them. I worked myself down until my body met his and stopped, resting my hands on his chest for balance and meeting his eyes. He looked so nervous as I leaned down and kissed him gently. Then I slowly rose up before dropping down to take all of him into me again. He cried out, grasping my hips, his nails digging into my skin. I moaned and started a steady pace. My head spun, and suddenly I was on my back, Markus driving into me faster. I cried out in bliss, wrapping my arms around him and clinging to him. I had been too caught up in the pleasure to think even once about how fast he'd changed our positions at the time. All I cared about was the pleasure and finally being one with the man of my dreams, the man that held my heart.

# Chapter 6

# Twisted Knife

*Present day*
*Ivan*

I was cold again, ice cold, as I went about my days alone. Things had gone bleak, the *life* just leached out of everything, as if Markus had been what embodied it all. With him gone, everything was just dull. Each morning, I had a cup of bitter black coffee and a slice of lightly buttered toast, then sat alone on my front porch. Normality, however bleak it was, at least satisfied my misery. I could no longer work, no longer do anything that would prevent atrophy, and I only accepted this because I would likely die before I had the chance.

This morning was different, however. My time on the porch was interrupted by an unexpected visitor. I knew he was bad news the second his car pulled up my long driveway and parked before the porch stairs, a sleek black machine meant to be fast and forgettable. The man that slid from the driver seat was just as sleek, like a panther that hunted for sport, dressed just as so in black leather and denim. His hair was shaved to scalp on both sides of his head, leaving a long length in the middle that extended back into a high ponytail. My eyes followed him as he climbed the stairs to my high porch, his gaze on his feet, but I knew he was focused on everything around him. It was when he reached the top step that his eyes met mine; and I knew who he was or, rather, what he did for a living. This man was most assuredly a vampire Hunter.

"Might I ask why you are trespassing on my property?" I said before he could speak, picking up my bitter coffee with the pretense of wanting to warm my hands though the coffee itself had long since gone cold from my lack of acknowledgement.

"You are Ivan Kristaski, right? Ex-lover of Markus Rose?" he asked in a deep voice that didn't bother to disguise its disgust.

"That would be me, but that also does not answer my question. Why are you here?" I asked, not bothering to disguise my own disdain at his presence now.

For the record, he was rude first.

"I've been sent to…hire you," he said simply, trying to deal his words carefully.

I had a feeling he wasn't quite like all slayers. He read as less brash, more manipulative than brute strength.

"Well, I am medically unfit for physical work. Sorry. Goodbye," I said dismissively.

I was not going to become a vampire Hunter. Were they nuts? Sure, I was angry with Markus. But I certainly didn't want to kill him.

"What you will be hired for is physical, yes, but not the kind that will endanger your life. It's a big proposal. Mind if I sit?" he asked, gesturing to Markus's—the only other empty chair.

"No, you will stand. I'll be refusing regardless, but I will pity you and listen," I said harshly, leaning back and crossing my arms.

The Hunter smirked, leaning against the railing instead and mimicking me, arms crossing over his muscled chest, revealing a torrent of scars lacing up his right arm.

"Fine then. I would assume you still care about that worthless leech you dumped. So I'm here to offer you a job where the pay will be his life. You will do as the Loremaster tells you, and the leech will live another day. Deny him, and he will be brought to you in pieces," he said darkly, giving no pause till the end.

My body jerked as if I'd been slapped. Markus. I couldn't let them kill Markus even if we weren't together anymore—even if I died. I couldn't let them kill him.

"Say I entertain this job offer, would it be promised that, if I die, he will forever be safe?" I asked, sounding more eager than I should have after the bastard had hurt me so deeply.

But I loved him too much to have him die due to my own actions and feeble life force.

"I'm sure you could work something out. So shall we go then?" he asked, pushing off the railing and walking toward the stairs.

"Wait…let me wash my dishes," I said, getting up and carrying my coffee cup in.

He rolled his eyes and followed me as I walked to the sink and filled it to wash the three coffee mugs and three butter knives that sat dirty in the sink.

"Does it matter? You probably won't be back here for a long while, if at all," the Hunter asked, leaning against the counter.

I shoved a dish towel into his hand and made him start drying dishes. Be useful, ya prick.

"It does because, if and when I die, this home goes to my best friend and her son. All of my assets do. So I'm not going to leave dirty dishes for them to deal with," I reasoned, washing the last knife and draining the sink.

"I suppose that makes sense. Now let's go," he said, grabbing my arm securely this time.

"Won't I need to bring some clothing?" I asked, hoping that this wasn't going to be a situation like my visit with the Weres.

"We will provide you with what clothing you will need," he said, not allowing me to stop this time as he just haphazardly dragged me to his car.

I sighed, giving one last look up at my old home and knew that, in a way, I was saying my goodbyes. I had a feeling this would be the last time I would see it in this life. I got in the passenger seat and pulled on the belt, not looking at the man sitting next to me. Instead, I closed my eyes and remembered, remembering the memories the old house held and biting back the tears this man didn't deserve to witness.

On Daniel's first birthday, cake smeared into the table as Miriam apologized profusely, and I just laughed away at the adorable boy. A fleeting memory of pushing back the furniture in the living room and learning to dance by myself. Hours spent studying on things that had momentarily caught my attention. Markus's lips on mine as we made out on the couch to the *Tokyo Ghoul* theme song. It was over, but the memories would be forever in my mind. I'd never forget them because they were the happiest moments of my life. They were times of both happiness and struggle, but that was life. Now…now I had to move on to the part where I'd meet my end. There was no way around it now, no avoiding it. I had to accept it now.

"Hey, I may be a dick in your eyes because my beliefs endanger yours, but I can feel your pain from here. Listen, I get the gist of what you will be doing there. So I am willing to be there if you need someone to…talk to. I can't tell you I'll be able to understand, but I can still be there," he said gently, stirring me from my memories.

I looked at him, noticing that he was texting and driving—with *my* phone!

"Hey! That is mine! And you're driving!" I exclaimed, trying to snatch my phone away.

"Chill, I'm a professional. Besides, you were out of it. That's why I decided I'd text your friend about your…vacation, which is what I've informed her. You've gone on to relieve some stress. By the way, my name is Zarrack," he said, deftly avoiding my grasping hands.

I flinched at the atrocious name.

"Sorry," I said.

He looked confused until he realized that I meant his name, and that had him laughing softly.

"Yeah, it's not ideal. But it is a name," he admitted, smiling sheepishly before relocking my phone and pocketing it.

"Do I not get it back?" I asked gently, trying to keep the comradery.

"You won't need it. I'm sorry. Just remember, I am just the messenger," Zarrack said as he pulled to the stop in front of a corporate building.

I swallowed. His words didn't leave me with a warm fuzzy feeling in the slightest.

"We're here," he said forebodingly.

I nodded, climbing out slowly and looking up at the building—Dark Horse Private Security Systems.

"I'm guessing this is just a front for vampire hunting?" I asked chokingly, nerves like knots as he got out and met me in front of the building.

"Yeah. Come on. May as well get this done," he said and led the way inside slowly.

I followed reluctantly, passing offices and conference rooms, locked doors, and more. Then we reached a pair of heavy double doors, metal and seemingly out of place. Zarrack paused and sighed, pushing the doors open and holding them open for me to walk through them. I walked in and froze at what I saw. It looked like an Egyptian brothel. Men and women, mostly men, lounged about in thin clothes and metal slave bands. I swallowed as one was pulled away behind a set of curtains that barely concealed their figures. Straight across from the doors was a throne like chair with a male sitting in it.

"That's the Loremaster. Go to him. He is your new boss," Zarrack said and backed out of the room as if the very thought of being in it disgusted him.

The doors clanged shut behind him, and I swallowed at the foreboding sound, walking hesitantly toward this "Loremaster."

"Hello, little Ivan. I am so glad you came willingly. Now you will be like these other men and women here at times. You will serve the Hunters and Weres that come through here. I am included in that tally. If we have other jobs for you, we will inform you of them. For now, you will go with Melissa here, and she will help you change," he said.

It was then that I fainted. Whether from stress, anxiety, or my own weakened body, I couldn't have been sure. Fuck you, Markus. I better hurry up and die.

*Markus*

I sighed quietly as I knocked on Miriam's apartment door, reluctant to see the woman who meant so much to Ivan. She had called and asked that I come over and babysit Daniel so she could go to work. I couldn't tell her no, not when I knew she was doing it so Ivan wouldn't be overstressed. Said woman opened the door a few seconds after my knock, smiling tiredly up at me. She was a small woman but taller than my Ivan.

"Good morning, Markus. I'm sorry for having to ask so last minute. I would've asked Ivan, but he went on vacation this morning and left me with no one to help me out at all," she said, pulling me inside quickly and grabbing up her keys, purse, and an old almost-gone tube of lip gloss.

"Wait, Ivy's on vacation?" I asked instantly.

It had been three weeks since we had split, and every second was painful. I loved that stupid, reckless man so much, so whenever Miriam had an update on him, I was willing to pry.

"Yeah. It was kinda surprising actually. He hadn't given any heads-up or told me he was planning anything, which is weird 'cuz he always tells me where he's going. I'm his proxy after all," she said softly, sighing and shrugging. "Anyways, I have to get going. I'll see you at nine tonight. I left some money on the counter for pizza 'cuz I haven't been able to go get groceries yet. I will pay you for taking care of him today. My number is on the fridge, along with his basic information in case of an emergency. Thank you again. I gotta go. I am running late," she added, kissing Danny's cheek and then my own before darting out the door.

I just stood there for a moment, frowning as I wondered what Ivan was doing. Where had he gone so suddenly and without warning? Why? I felt a little tug on my hand and forced myself to smile down at Danny.

"Hey, buddy. Wanna go play some video games at Uncle Ivan's?" I asked him gently, smiling softly.

I could do a little snooping and see if I could turn something up and keep the boy entertained while I was at it.

"Yeah!" Danny exclaimed, beaming excitedly and rushing to get his shoes on.

The boy reminded me so much of Ivan. I guess spending so much time with him had rubbed off on the impressionable youth.

I grabbed his coat and helped him put it on, then grabbed the spare car seat out of the closet. Taking his hand, we walked out to my car, and I got him secured in. He stopped my hands when I tried to buckle him up, and I frowned until he exclaimed.

"I can do it!" And he buckled himself in.

I looked up at him and looked into his soft green eyes. He'd probably gotten those eyes from his father. His mother certainly didn't have them. He probably got the wavy hair from him too though the color was all Miriam. He really was an adorable boy, intelligent too. Once he was buckled, I got in the driver seat and started for Ivan's place, the old house on the outskirts of town. He'd stayed after his uncle's death because he so adored the privacy and nature that surrounded it.

"If I want company, I will seek it. But home is for peace," he had said. It had been something I had loved about him. He was an introvert but could be social when he needed to.

"Do you think Uncle Ivan is okay? Everything has been so… crazy lately. I don't understand a lot 'cuz I'm little. But I know something is up. I'm not stupid…no…naive. That's the word, right, Uncle Markus?" Danny piped up, startling me with his questions.

"Yeah, that's the word. And I'm sure Uncle Ivy is fine. He's just going through a lot right now," I said, smiling at him in the rearview mirror.

But his expression told me he didn't quite believe it.

"All right…," he said despite his apprehension, sounding just like Ivan when he didn't believe a word you'd said.

They both worry too much. I pulled into Ivan's driveway and was startled to find his beloved car still there. But perhaps he'd taken a cab so his car wouldn't get damaged in the airport parking lot—if he even took a plane. I parked next to his car and got out, peeking inside, but didn't find anything out of order. I turned and opened the door, helping Danny out and holding his hand as we went inside. He chattered away, sounding like a little boy again. Inside, I set him down in front of the huge TV in the living room and got him playing a Pokémon game.

Once he was sufficiently distracted, I went back on the porch. It was where Ivan's scent had been the freshest. But that wasn't what had pulled me there. It was the familiar tainted and metallic scent of a Hunter that did. I followed the scent to just before Ivan's chair, where it glanced mine and seeped into the kitchen and back. Their scents became mixed as though they had walked together from the kitchen and off the porch. This made me nervous. What would a Hunter want with my Ivan, or had Ivan contacted him to end me? Though, I doubted Ivan was so angry with me to want me killed. I went back inside and upstairs, getting more nervous as I found his suitcase still in the closet and all of his clothes still in his closet and dresser. He'd left with the Hunter and hadn't come back. He'd gone on "vacation" with a Hunter and not a stitch of luggage. I had to look more into this for his sake and mine.

*Ivan*

I was behind one of those stupid curtains, straddling Zarrack's clothed lap, pretending to be grinding for any prying eyes. I had been in the brothel for two weeks now, and I was exhausted from being the toy for any Hunter who needed their rocks off. Zarrack was a different story. He was my informant and my "partner" when I was sent to do the Loremaster's dirty work.

"You really don't feel anything when I do this?" I asked him gently as I put a little actual pressure into the grinding over him, curious of my pin-straight friend.

"It's not that I feel nothing. I'm not dead from the waist down. I just don't like men. It's pleasant because you are very good at that. But I feel nothing for you, no offense," Zarrack replied softly, smiling a bit. "We're not here for you to discuss my sexuality. I'm here to tell you about your pet parasite," he added, poking fun at the fact that Markus was a vampire.

"Yes, that is true. How is he? Healthy, I hope," I asked softly, easing back on the grinding so it was fake again.

These sessions were times for my body to rest, per Zarrack's insistence after finding me bleeding and covered in bruises the first time he'd come with information.

"He is. He is worried about you, of course. He's been taking care of your friend's little boy at your house. He knows something is up with your disappearance and blames himself," he said softly, lying back on the cushions, his expression distraught.

"Poor Markus. I wish I could see him," I murmured softly, climbing up off his lap and pulling him to his feet, pretending to give him a kiss.

"I know. I feel bad for you," he said, rubbing the back of his neck softly. "I have to go though. Take it easy. I heard Yuuta was talking about coming here to enjoy his favorite 'redheaded slut.' Since you're the only redhead in the brothel, I'm guessing that's you," he said, stepping out of the curtains.

"Yeah. He is actually surprisingly gentle for the muscle-bound freak he is. I'm thinking he needs some help with his home life. He's lacking the passion he's trying to get from me," I explained, following him out as I pretended to be fixing my loin sash, the metal rings on my arms and neck clinking because they couldn't find ones that were tight enough to sit flush against my skin.

"I can see that, honestly. He doesn't seem to have anyone to come home to, at least not that I have noticed. See you tomorrow," he said, smiling gently and leaving the brothel.

He himself had told me that the brothel made his skin crawl, disgusted him to no end. He hated the road the slayers were going down. He would make a good leader if there was ever a revolution. I wouldn't live to see it, but that was fine. It wasn't mine to see.

I got into a sort of lounging position on my cushions. The room was split into six different "toys" that could move about the room freely and socialize with each other. There was a table of refreshments that was heated and fresh for us. It seemed luxurious on the outside, but we were all there due to blackmail. We were all the lovers or ex-lovers of vampires. In order to protect our loved ones, we were being forced to whore ourselves out for the ones that would kill them if we didn't. Out of the six of us, only two of us were women. Mikayla and Lilly were sweet and strong, but both had a hard time with the job. They had to risk getting pregnant with a slayer's baby. I couldn't blame them. I wouldn't want to be carrying Yuuta's spawn; that was for sure.

I was shaken from my thoughts as I was suddenly dragged to my feet by hair, biting my lip on the strangled yelp that tried to escape my mouth. I was brought face-to-face with my most hated, despised customer, those unforgettable purple eyes that had held the controller to the shock collar. He was always great for insults and left me covered in blood and bruises, so I would have to go bathe before I could rest. It was the most frustrating thing, especially when he liked it fast, rough, and with little prep.

"Hello, Lukai," I said carefully, trying not to piss him off too quickly.

After learning the name of this monster, it was hard to not say it with venom.

"Shut up, fang fucking slut. Go get in there and get disrobed. I want you now. No hesitation," he growled, throwing me toward my set of curtains.

I skidded but managed to stay on my feet. Someone was already in a foul mood and was going to take it out on me. I swallowed, holding my head high as I walked behind the curtain and dropped my loin sash. I was suddenly shoved facedown into the cushions.

"Lukai…please use the lube. You don't have to prepare me. But please don't thrust in dry this time. I have other clients to tend to other than you," I said, swallowing as I got an idea. "You're my favorite, of course, but the others use me too. The Loremaster is getting angry about it. You don't want him to restrict my use now, do you?" I purred, wiggling my ass seductively in hopes of bringing my point across despite the disgust coiling in my stomach.

"Fine, but only because you asked so prettily," he said, easing the pressure on my head as he reached to grab one of many types of bottles of lube.

I heard the bottle snap open and knew he was lubing up his average-sized cock. His words made me sick, reminding me too much of Markus's flirting. I relaxed as best as I could, feeling sick to my stomach, missing my Markus, and hating this violation.

"I love the way you do me, Lukai," I said, fighting the urge to gag on my words as he pressed his slickened cock against my tight ass and started his hurried penetration, none too gentle.

But the lube eased the pain a little bit, my body forced open roughly. Lukai grunted and groaned, hands on my hips as he lay against my hips, his own thrusting roughly.

"You feel so good inside…You're so soft and dainty…I know you like me better than your vamp. Say it! Tell me I'm better than that vampire, and I'll make you mine. You'll be my special little toy, and no one can touch you but me," he purred in my ear, making my stomach roll.

I couldn't say that. I wouldn't. He could be as rough and horrible as he wanted, and I would never spew such a toxic lie.

"No…you're not…Just fuck me and leave…or I'll report you to the Loremaster, and he'll believe me because he knows that I am honest and don't lie," I growled, then yelped when he bit down hard on my shoulder and kicked his thrusts into overdrive.

But at this point, I was loose enough that it only pulled tortured moans from my throat.

"You're doing this all in vain. Your lover will be killed regardless of your attempts to save him. The other five are here with no knowledge that their lovers are dead and gone. Eliminated. When he is killed, I will claim you as mine, and you will never ever leave my bed until the day you die," he threatened in my ear.

I went stock-still before fainting once again. I knew, when I would come to, I would be battered, sore, and messy. But my mind had already shut down from panic.

# Chapter 7

# Another Hospital and an Unexpected Partnership

*Ivan*

I woke to soft sheets and warm clothes and, for a moment, thought I was back home. But then, I felt the pangs of violent sex and remembered what had happened before I had passed out. After a few moments, I managed to crack open my eyelids. The room I was in was pale white and reminded me of my hospital room. I moved to sit up slowly, groaning as I did, feeling the bruises on my hips and the damage to my poor asshole with every small movement. I really needed to stop waking up like this.

"Oh, you're awake," a soft voice murmured.

I turned my head to see Zarrack stepping into the room.

"Zarrack! Get away from me, you fucking traitor," I said, feeling the anger surge in me.

He had lied to me from the very beginning. They were still going to kill Markus. He had promised me that being here would keep them from killing him. I had degraded and dirtied myself for nothing.

"Haha. Right, Ivan. I'm glad you're awake. Your liver was acting up, so we were concerned you'd go into a coma," he said with a soft laugh as he plopped down in the chair next to me.

"I'm serious! You're a liar, a traitor, and a murderer!" I exclaimed, tears welling in my eyes.

Zarrack looked at me, frowning.

"What? Did I do something and not realize it?" Zarrack asked, frown deepening as the tears spilled down my face.

"You lied to me! They're just going to kill him anyway! I'm doing this all for nothing! All of us in the brothel are! The others have already lost their lovers and don't even know it yet!" I exclaimed, glaring at him, my weak body trembling with anger and hatred.

A jolt ran through Zarrack's form, his eyes widening as his breath caught in his throat. Real or not, I could see horror in his eyes at my words.

"I never lied to you. I keep tabs on the bloodsucker for you! I hate liars, and I believe that some vamps are good and don't necessarily need to be killed. Markus is alive and well. I don't know about the rest of them, but I know he is alive," Zarrack said roughly, standing, grabbing my shoulders, and squeezing.

I yelped and glared softly, shoving at him.

"Get off of me! Lukai himself told me that they're going to kill him anyway and that, once he is gone, Lukai is going to make me his personal fuck toy!" I exclaimed angrily.

Trembles wracked my body as I imagined being trapped as Lukai's toy forever. My body would be broken, bruised, and battered until I died unless I could keep him manipulated gently.

"Then I'll make sure that never happens. I'll figure something out. But for now...I'll pay off the nurse to keep you here," he said, patting my shoulder gently and nodding before darting off, holding a fury I'd never seen in him before.

I still wasn't sure I could believe him. He was still a Hunter after all.

*Zarrack*

The rage that had filled me when Ivan told me what Lukai had told him was unlike any I had ever felt. I had long since believed our people's mission had become perverted and skewed, but to go so far as to lie to your own people, it was unforgivable. They knew that I would never agree to this callous injustice. Those men and women had given up everything to save their loved ones. They had left their homes, their families, and their lives as human beings all with the promise that it would protect those they had been forced to leave behind.

I found myself picking the lock to the file room that the Loremaster himself told me was for things that didn't concern me. I didn't know what I would find there but knew, if I were to be caught in here, my punishment would be severe. But I had to find out what my people were hiding from me. With a heavy heart, I slipped inside the room and jammed the door shut with a bookshelf from beside the door. There were ten filing cabinets and a desktop computer in the dusty old room. I slowly approached the desk, checking the room for cameras and grinding my teeth when I found one glaring back at me. I picked up the desk chair and threw it with all of my strength, satisfied by the crunch of glass and plastic that followed. Turning to the desk, I saw a single plain manila folder next to the keyboard. I picked it up, and my heart sank as I read the name neatly printed on the tab: Ivan Kristaski. With a deep strengthening breath, I opened the file. What I saw inside made my stomach roll, and I dropped the file, running to the trash can to promptly lose lunch.

Finished being sick, I shakily returned to pick the file folder up from the floor, gathering the photos that had scattered when I'd dropped it. The photo that had made me so sick glared back at me… Ivan hanging from the ceiling with blood pouring down his back. This hadn't been taken here; I knew that for a fact. But I had seen Ivan's scars. We had done this, or our allies had. Ivan was a human. How could we do this to a human? We'd sworn oaths to protect them, and they meant nothing. I closed the file and tucked it into the bag I'd brought with me. I wasn't done snooping. If this was here, there had to be more on the others, and I *was* going to find it.

*Markus*

I sat alone in Ivan's house, crying yet again as my emotions ate at me. I needed to get a hold of myself. I had an eternity left to live. I knew this was an eventuality, that the time would come when we would be no more. I just never expected it to be so soon and so painful. This whole lifetime of experience went so unexpectedly it fell apart so quickly.

I was pulled from my thoughts by the front door opening and footsteps echoing down the hall toward me. I frowned and stood, panicking and expecting it to be Ivan. But the being that appeared in the doorway was a human I recognized by scent alone. I growled instinctively and surged forward, expecting him to use his Hunter training to dodge or counter my attack. But he let me shove him against the wall with a hand to his throat.

"Where is he?" I snarled, feeling my rage surge in my chest at his very presence and Ivan's lack thereof.

"He is safe, for now. I need you to calm down and let me talk. He sent me here, sort of. So let me down. I'll make some coffee, and we can talk this through. There is a lot going on that you don't know, and we need to work together in order to stop it," he said, struggling to talk around my grasp but still forced the words out anyway.

"How do I know I can trust you? For all I know, this is some elegant trick by the Hunters to get to me!" I exclaimed, trembling in my anger.

He scoffed and reached up, grasping my wrist tightly. Using that alone, he pushed himself up off the wall and eased my grip up off his throat. He was very strong, even for a Hunter.

"Like they would send me for such a thing. My acting sucks," he said and walked lithely toward the kitchen, seeming to know where everything was, at least enough to make the coffee.

I followed him hesitantly, watching him closely.

"Is he…all right…healthy?" I forced out, wanting to test his knowledge of my little love, truly concerned for him.

"Honestly it's not looking good for him. He's in a private hospital right now. I was afraid he was going to go into a coma. But he is strong. Even though he's ceased to hold a will to live, he's considerably strong," he responded, his back to me as he worked, starting the coffeemaker and turning to look at me.

He leaned back against the counter, looking me over as if surveying my reaction to his words. I felt my mouth go dry at his words, my heart thudding in my chest. My Ivy…in another hospital. He hates hospitals so much; he'd told me so himself.

"So"—I swallowed around, the knot growing in my throat—"what do you mean he sent you here 'sort of'?" I asked, worried about my poor Ivy in the hands of the Hunters.

"He doesn't know I've come to you. He knows I've been observing you, making sure you are alive and well. At his request, might I add. He knows you are in some form of danger that not even I knew of. That is, until I went snooping in the confidential file room," he said, taking the drawstring bag off his back and opening it.

I automatically tensed, a defensive growl curling from my lips. He froze and blinked, looking up at me and laughing.

"Chill, fang face. I'm not going to hurt you. I'm practically unarmed. I'm doing this for Ivan. He's a good man. He's a better man than most of the slayers I work with. The disgusting things they've done to him…," he trailed off with a shiver, looking appalled as he pulled open the bag and slapped a stack of manila folders down on the kitchen table.

I couldn't look at him, feeling choked by his words.

"What have they done to him!" I shouted, resisting the urge to grab his shoulders and shake the answers out of him.

"I'm not going to tell you. I need you clearheaded, and you won't be if I describe those atrocities. You'll already learn enough from these files. I need you to remember. You can't help him if you're out of your mind with worry or rage. Now sit. Read through those files while I fix the coffee. I was sick reading through those myself. How do you take your coffee?" he asked me gently, pulling a chair out for me before pulling down a couple of coffee mugs and the tin of sugar.

"Uh…three scoops of sugar. The spoon Ivy uses should still be in the tin," I said, angling the chair so I could keep my eyes on him.

He simply nodded, giving me his back again as he started mixing up the coffees. He was either overly trusting or overly confident that he could take me if I wanted to attack him. I swallowed and turned to the files on the table. There were six with names evenly printed on the tabs in permanent marker. I picked up the top file, reading the name on the tab. Gavin Maverick. Sounded like a rock star's name. I opened the file and was greeted to a profile of sorts on Gavin, as well as a small grouping of photos. I set the photos aside without looking at them, interested in the information on the profile paper. There was a photo taped in the top right corner looking almost like a mug shot. The man looked back at me from the page with a stricken, sorrowful expression. His short black hair was hanging just long enough to be in his face, but he didn't seem to be able to brush it back before the photo was taken, his soft brown eyes reflecting such deep sorrow. I swallowed painful, imagining poor Ivan looking the same way.

I tore my eyes away from the photo and moved on to the document's contents, the words typed neatly across the page. It was like a demented version of a dating profile, lacking any emotion or effort.

Name: Gavin Maverick
Age: 24
Height: 5'8"
Weight: 200 lbs.
Eyes: Brown
Hair: Black
Race: Caucasian
Details: Has a small tattoo on his hip of a realistic heart. Has the tip of his cock pierced. Has a fear of tight spaces and deep homophobia. Ex-lover of Valon Merk.
Status of wife: Terminated

I choked as I read the word *terminated*. It was listed so heartlessly, the murder of someone easily filed and forgotten. Did Gavin know? Why was this Hunter showing me these things? I jolted when said Hunter appeared in my view, setting the coffee down on the table in front of me, a hand on my shoulder to steady himself. It was so mundane and harmless. He seemed so harmless I had forgotten he was even there. He must have felt me tense because he eased back and stopped touching me.

"Sorry. I really mean you no harm. I forget that my presence unnerves anyone with a pair of fangs. Listen, I have one weapon, and it's a sword down my back underneath the leather straps. I have it snapped in place, so I can't draw it easily. It's made like that so it won't fly out when I'm on my motorcycle. If it will make you feel better...I will give it to you until you trust me enough to give it back. I really just want to help Ivan, and if it means going completely unarmed, well, so be it," the Hunter said, reaching back to something behind his neck.

I heard snaps come loose, and he carefully drew a beautiful, well-kept blade from a sheath hidden along his spine. He laid it gently on the table in front of me. I swallowed, shocked by this act. No slayer went unarmed in the company of a vampire. He could be lying, but something told me to trust him.

"What's your name?" I asked, trying to play nice for Ivan's sake. He looked startled, then smiled gently.

"It's Zarrack. Zarrack Goldguild. Now read. I'll answer any questions with whatever knowledge I have. We have time. However much he hates it, I paid for him to be kept in the hospital longer than necessary. He's safer there, much safer," he said gently.

I nodded and looked down at the photos that had accompanied the file. The top file showed Gavin stretched out on a pile of cushions, dressed in little more than scraps of fabric and hunks of metal. It barely covered him, especially in the position he lounged in. I flipped to the next photo and jolted. It was pornographic in every sense of the word. Gavin was pinned on his back, his wrists bound over his head while a Hunter stood between his legs, inside him. Blood trickled out of him and down his legs. His expression was one of pain, fear, and reluctant pleasure as the brute over him had him by his cock, which was, indeed, pierced at the tip. I gagged and threw the pictures back in the folder without even peeking at the others.

"Are they doing this...to my Ivy?" I asked, voice choked as I glanced up at him.

Afraid of his answer, I shakily gulped the coffee, which was still hot enough to sear my mouth.

"Yes…but not as roughly. He's good at manipulating his abusers into being gentler than usual. But that's why he's safer in the hospital. I've never approved of the way my people are going. But it's the last step that they would lie to me, one of their own, in order to get what they want. This is wrong. I want to take them out…end this tyranny now. We as a people were originally formed to only take out vampires that were dangerous to humanity. It's in the ancient texts. I am a good student. I've learned my history well. I want to put it back the way it was. I know it's hard, but keep reading. Ivan's file is there too, unfortunately," he said.

I felt my chest constrict. I was so wrong letting him go. The next time he asked, I would turn him without a fight. I wasn't going to lose him ever again after this—if he even wanted me back. It was my fault he was there, my fault the Hunters' attention was turned to him.

I picked up the next file, reading the next name. Mikayla Haven. I looked at the woman in the mugshot-like photo, noting she looked pissed off and roughed up. Her soft blond hair was messed up around her face, her dark-blue eyes glaring at me from the page. I was surprised the page hadn't burst into flame from the heat of her gaze. I continued on to the information on the page, so tense my shoulders hurt.

Name: Mikayla Haven
Age: 32
Height: 4'11"
Weight: 90 lbs.
Eyes: Blue
Hair: Blonde
Race: Caucasian
Details: Scar on leg from past surgery. Feisty. Wife of Finney.
Status of Husband: Terminated

I frowned, beginning to see a pattern in the mates of these humans. They had all been murdered, I would assume, except for me. I swallowed, shutting the file without even trying to look at the stack of accompanying photos. Last thing I wanted to see was a woman forced into the same position as Gavin had been. The photos should be burned. No one should have to see their humiliation. Zarrack stayed quiet, sipping his coffee and watching me. I'd become more relaxed, feeling like he was my ally, not my enemy. I was glad that he was there for Ivan and glad he had our backs. I flipped to the next folder, feeling a frustrated sigh slide past my lips. Did I want to see Ivan's, or was I stalling? My chest tightened every time I moved on to a new folder. Part of me wanted to see him, but the other part didn't want to witness what he had gone through. Was that selfish, sparing myself the pain by avoiding his?

Lilly Garrick was the name on the tab as I opened the file. This one didn't have a profile. I was simply met with a barrage of photos and a printed copy of an email saying that her fiancée was "taken care of." The photos were a mix of dirty, sexual acts and poses of a thin Black woman with cropped hair and of a very murdered female vampire. I gagged and took off, barely making it to the bathroom before I vomited the partially digested mac and cheese from dinner with Danny last night. This was sick, but I had to keep going. Knowledge was power, and I needed a lot of it right now, especially if I was going to rescue Ivan.

I stood from kneeling over the toilet and flushed the sick away, steeling myself. I was going to read Ivan's folder and put the rest away. This was for Ivan. I couldn't let myself be shaken off by disgusting photographs.

*Ivan*

I woke slowly, unsure what it was that had caused me to stir. My eyes cracked open, and I looked around the room, slowly focusing on Yuuta standing at the foot of the bed. I jolted up, shocked by his presence. It sent an instant nervous thrill through me.

"Yu-Yuuta...I can't service you today...I was severely damaged," I said, gritting my teeth at my words, sounding robotic, a broken product.

I pulled my knees up to my chest as he came closer, my heart racing in my chest.

"Sh, I'm not here to hurt you. I heard what Lukai did to you. I'm so sorry, little one. You are there to take care of our needs, and he abused you so horribly. It was wrong. But I took care of it for you, sweet one. He'll keep his hands off of you now," Yuuta said, holding up his hands.

They were wrapped tightly in bandages, a little blood seeping to the surface. I felt my eyes widen in surprise. He had beaten up Lukai for me. He called it abuse, not damage. He didn't think of me as a product. I felt tears prick my eyes, and a sob escaped my chest.

"You shouldn't have done that...It won't matter...Nothing matters...," I choked out, my arms so tight around my legs that my feet were tingling.

Yuuta looked at me, seeming stricken by the tears in my eyes, and leaned forward, hesitantly rubbing my back.

"I did it because you are so good to me. I know you were forced into this and had no choice. But you don't fight as long as I'm gentle and careful. I don't want to hurt you. You are so delicate, breakable. I can see what that vampire of yours sees in you," he said gently, carefully easing up onto the side of the bed so he could give me a gentle hug.

I tensed, then lay back into him gently, deciding to trust him. He was right. He'd never purposely tried to hurt me. Even with his terrifying stature, he tried to never hurt me.

"I wish there were more like you. It would make the job a little easier," I said with a humorless laugh.

"Tell me who hurts you, and I'll protect you from them. I swear it," he said sincerely, gripping my arm and resting his chin on my head, just holding me.

It felt nice. I hadn't been held in so long. He wasn't my Markus, but he was warm and kind. If I died here, I was glad I had Yuuta, I decided.

"I will…some days…I wish I could just sleep through it," I admitted, feeling loose-lipped. Maybe it was something in the IV. "Even without the pain, most of the time, I don't come. I don't have to for them to be satisfied," I muttered bitterly.

"Selfish. They're selfish. I've been selfish too, haven't I? I'll make it up to you. How are you feeling now?" he asked.

I felt a blush creep up my face. Was he serious?

"I…uh…can't do any penetration for another several days…," I managed, almost shy with it.

I had never been shy, but the scars and experiences made me a hell of lot more modest than I had ever been.

"But it won't hurt you if I were to touch you elsewhere?" he asked bluntly, his hands stayed holding me gently.

He wasn't already touching me sexually. He was giving me a choice. What did he want to do? Touch me while he jerked it?

"As long as you avoid the bruises, it shouldn't," I said hesitantly, wondering why I was so willingly answering his questions.

"Then I am asking you, not as a servant here, but as a human being with free will. Do you want me to touch you to pleasure you? I won't be selfish with you anymore," he said, still holding, truly letting me make the decision.

I swallowed, my mouth suddenly very dry.

"Yes, please, Yuuta. I'm tired of feeling only numbness and pain," I said softly, blushing brightly.

He nodded above me, his chin still on my head. He seemed to give me a moment more to think about what I agreed to before gently moving a hand up to untie the back of my hospital gown. His calloused hands rasped against my skin as he slid the gown down my arms, sending a shiver throughout my body. The gown was pulled carefully off of me and tossed into the chair beside the bed.

"So beautiful," he purred, leaning down and laying a soft kiss against my neck before drawing back and looking over my body.

His big, calloused hands were ever so gentle as they trailed over every inch of my bare skin, pausing on bruises that made him look angry for a moment. He seemed especially angered by the hand-shaped bruises on my hips and thighs. Then his eyes caught the brand mark in my skin, his fingers tracing over the deep older scar.

"This is Lukai's Hunter mark. When did he do this to you? It's not recent enough to have been done here," he growled softly.

I swallowed, startled by his angry questions.

"The weres captured me before I came here. Lukai was with them. He is the cause of the brand and a few of the other older scars," I muttered as I turned slightly to him, flinching at the pang of pain that cut through my lower half with the movement.

But I didn't let it hinder me as I cupped his face and placed a soft kiss on his lips. This seemed to surprise him, but he melted into the kiss for a moment, covering my hands with his. Then he gently sat me back, shaking his head.

"You are so kind, Yuuta. Why can I not kiss you?" I asked softly, frowning at him.

"This is about your pleasure, little one. I can't lose my mind to you and your sweet little kisses, especially because losing control could hurt you further. There will be time for sweet kisses when you are healed," he said, his breathing ragged.

Did he truly mean to just pleasure me and receive nothing in return? I blushed deeply.

"All…all right," I said softly and slowly slid my hands off his face.

He nodded, swallowing softly and placing a kiss to my brow, slowly easing further up onto the bed, and stopping to unlace his heavy boots and kick them off. Then he positioned himself between my legs on his elbows, gently easing my legs apart. Another frown graced his face as he caught sight of the bloodied bandages that protected my damaged anus.

"I'm sorry I didn't come to your rescue," he said gruffly as if he were fighting off tears.

He then leaned in, slowly kissing up my thigh toward my cock, which was only semihard. The closer his kisses came to it, the harder it became. The position he'd put me was the least painful and made it easier to get excited. Instead of touching my cock, he slid to my other thigh, his hot lips trailing up my skin again and his tongue darting against my flesh from time to time. I felt my breath speed, my arousal making my cock twitch expectantly, wanting to be touched. But I was patient—for now anyway.

"Mmph…tease…," I said, hearing the breathiness of my own voice, the impatience.

Well, I tried. Yuuta chuckled quietly against my skin, his mouth on my inner thigh, so very close to that hard wanton part of me.

"Your impatience is cute. But I'll indulge you," he said softly, smiling up at me as a lock of his long black hair slid free of his ponytail and graced his cheek.

He was very handsome. In another world, I could probably run with him. But it wasn't in the cards.

I was pulled from my thoughts by my own soft gasp as I felt his hot tongue on my sensitive cock, from base to tip in a slow motion that left me twitching. Fuck, for a top, he was good at that. His tongue circled the tip of my cock and swirled all the way down, making my hips jerk as my hands dug into the sheets. He hadn't even put me in his mouth yet, and I was already a twitchy mess. It had been so long since I'd been allowed to seek my own pleasure my body was wicked sensitive. I felt his hands strongly pin my hips but not enough to bruise, pointedly avoiding the bruises I already wore.

"Hold on, little one," he purred.

I looked at him questioningly. But those questions were answered as his lips engulfed my twitching cock, and my back arched, a soft cry spilling from my lips as I clutched at the sheets. Fuck, hot. Was I seeing stars from just this? How hard up was I? My thoughts scattered as he started to bob his head along my length, his tongue working along my flesh easily. His eyes were on my face, watching my reactions as I writhed beneath his actions. One of his hands slid off my hip and trailed to my balls, hand caressing gently, sending hot jolts of pleasure through my heated body. My hips bucked softly, wanting more, and he released my hip, suckling me hard as I bucked again hesitantly. He drew up off me, and I whimpered softly until he kissed the tip of my cock with a smile.

"Wha—?" I started but was cut off as he massaged my balls softly, sending a lance of pleasure through me.

"Buck as much as you like, little one. You won't hurt me. This pleasure is yours as you want it," he murmured, voice raspy with lust.

Then his lips were over me again, and I let out a low moan, shuddering. His tongue lapped along my cock, and another moan spilled from me. My hips jerked as he sucked sharply; and I did as he said, letting my body thrust carefully up between his lips, the sensation prying another sound from me. I was already so close.

*Just a little more* was all I could think as my brain went mushy with pleasure.

My hips moved at an even rhythm, broken only by Yuuta's sucking that left my head spinning.

"Ah! I...I am close!" I managed to stutter out, my grip on the sheets making my knuckles go white and my thrusts moving faster.

Yuuta looked up at me, his golden-brown eyes locking with mine as he suddenly suckled hard and fast on me. That was all it took as I came hotly, my hips thrusting my cock to the hilt in his mouth. He grasped my hips, holding me there as he swallowed quickly, a blush gracing his face. I shuddered as my body went slack, my chest rising and falling fast as I struggled to catch my breath. He slowly drew off of me and leaned over me. I felt my breath catch in my throat, terror consuming me automatically as I thought he wanted to continue with my damaged body. But he simply kissed up my neck to my lips, kissing me gently with the taste of me still on his tongue, my cheeks reddening.

"So beautiful," he murmured, caressing my cheek gently before standing and grasping up my gown. "Let me get you a clean one and maybe the nurse. I wanna make sure you aren't hurt by this," he said thoughtfully, turning to walk away, but I caught his arm gently.

"You'll come back, right? If you're not busy...I would love it if you could lie with me...until I fall asleep?" I asked him softly.

Was I the one being selfish now, wanting to take him away from his life just to hold me? I just felt so vulnerable and emotional. I need the support of someone who cares, if only for a few moments.

"I will. I want to learn how to bandage you so you don't have to worry about everyone else seeing you this way. I'll take care of you, Ivan," he said.

My heart clenched as he spoke my name for the first time. I wasn't a nameless slut to him. I was somebody to him. With my nod, he slipped out of the room, leaving me lying there, satisfied and grateful. Then the tears came.

# Chapter 8

# Death and Sex

*Markus*

When I'd returned to the kitchen, Zarrack had swept all the files up off the table but for one, stuffing them back into the bag. He'd left his sword on the table and had gone to refill his coffee, his back to me yet again.

"Read the file. It's Ivan's. It's far more graphic, just to warn you. After this, we need to come up with a plan and find allies," he said as I walked back into the room.

Then he turned toward me fast, eyes over my shoulder, just as I heard the sound of someone shuffling toward me from behind.

"Duck!" he said.

I did so without thinking as he suddenly whipped a kitchen knife past my head. There was a muted thump, then a thud. I turned and found the body of a Were on the floor behind me, the knife sticking out of his forehead. I gasped softly, startled by this. Had he just saved me by killing a beast that was supposed to be his ally?

"What the…Why did you…?" I stuttered out, looking at him as he walked past me to yank the knife out of his skull and carry it to the sink.

"Just take the body out back and burn it. Once you're done, we're leaving. It's not safe here anymore," he said, turning on the sink and washing the knife without looking at me.

I nodded and picked up the body, hefting it up over my shoulder and heading out back. What kind of mess was this becoming? This wasn't me, willingly burning a body. Killing had never been my thing, but doing it to protect Ivan was different. I could do this. I had to because Ivan was counting on me.

*Ivan*

I woke slowly in a warm embrace, locks of soft black hair mingling with my red ones across my face, and I knew I lay in Yuuta's bed in his quarters. He'd paid the nurse off to keep up the ruse that I was healing while allowing him to take me to his room. That nurse was gonna be one rich bitch if people kept paying her off for me. It had been almost a week since Zarrack had come to see me, and I explained to Yuuta what he was doing for me, partially to keep him from beating him up. He knew he was a "regular" of mine, just not that he was pin straight and simply my informant. Now I lay naked in his bed with him spooned against my back. He wore a pair of pajama pants and held me close. Despite the nurse giving the go-ahead for penetration again, he continued to insist upon my pleasure alone. I stirred, moving to slip out of his arms, and felt them tighten around me.

"Good morning, Ivan," he murmured, placing a kiss on my neck before letting me go.

I got up slowly and smiled softly at him.

"I'm gonna shower. Care to join me?" I asked softly, blushing lightly.

This was normal, right? I used to say the same thing to Markus. Did Yuuta know me well enough to know I was going to try to seduce him into sex? I was healed enough to do it, and I wanted the pleasure to be mutual again. It felt so wrong to just take and take when he was so kind to me.

"Mm…nice try, little hot brand. No," he said soft and firmly as he sat up and stretched, his hair falling loosely around his shoulders.

"Please, let me give back to you. I miss having you inside me. You've been so attentive to me," I said, climbing back onto the bed and straddling his clothed lap, grasping his face gently and kissing him sweetly.

He kissed me back softly, his hands coming to rest on my hips, the bruises faded, almost gone now.

"All right. But only because I can't tell you no when you make that face," he murmured, nipping my shoulder as he picked me up and carried me toward his bathroom.

I blushed softly, forgetting how strong he was, not that it took much to carry my delicate frame. He brought me in and set me on a towel on the sink counter, licking my neck softly before moving to play with the taps. I leaned back on the counter, watching him. I could feel a migraine growing behind my eyes, a regular occurrence these days, as well as the almost-feverish skin; but I didn't let it deter me.

Once the shower was going, Yuuta turned to me and pulled his shirt off, walking up to stand between my legs. I eagerly met him in a soft kiss, his teeth nipping at my lip so I would open my mouth. I parted my lips, my tongue meeting his in a tantalizing dance. He tasted so good, his hands so gentle as he grasped my hips. The room began to fill with steam from the shower, sticking to our bodies as we continued our heated kiss. I don't know how he managed to strip off the rest of his clothes, but he was naked as he carried me into the warm streams of water. He groaned softly, pressing me gently against the wall, tensing when I jolted from the cold tiles. I stopped his worry with a deep kiss as he carefully set me down on the floor of the shower, sliding his hands along my skin as the water coated us. I pulled back from his lips, panting softly as I placed my hands on his chest, pushing him under the water so his long black locks became soaked, sticking to his skin. I ran my hands along his muscular chest and slowly started to slip to my knees until he grasped my arm to stop me.

"You don't have to do that," he panted softly, blushing.

I smiled, gently grasping and stroking his cock. He moaned lowly but held tightly onto my arm.

"I told you I want you inside of me, and water alone doesn't work as a lube," I said heatedly, happy when he released me.

I eased down on my knees, gently nuzzling against his cock and looking up at him seductively. His breath seemed to catch in his throat, and he caressed my face.

"So beautiful," he purred as I lapped softly up the length of his cock and then closed my lips over the head, making him jerk and moan.

He held my head, caressing my hair as I took him in my mouth, my tongue licking softly.

"Urgh…that's enough. Kiss me," he groaned, pulling me up so his cock slid out of my mouth.

I pouted at him, and he let out a shaky laugh.

"Hmph…fine," I purred softly and kissed him deeply, my tongue lashing with his.

His cock was a little smaller than Markus, and I could take him with little preparation. So Yuuta would be just as easy. He smiled, kissing me back deeply as he lifted one of my legs, pressing the head against my entrance.

"Ready for me?" he asked gently.

I nodded eagerly. With that, he supported my body by my leg and a hand on my hip, pushing slowly into me. I groaned softly, throwing my arms around his neck with a soft cry.

"Mmph, I forgot…how good you feel…," he panted as he worked his way inside me, moving in slow thrusts that stretched me open around him.

I moaned, clinging to him as he finally filled me to the hilt and stopped for a moment, resting inside me for a moment.

"I've missed this," I moaned. "You don't have to be overly gentle. I'll let you know if you're hurting me," I said, twisting my hips on him, making him moan softly.

"All right, thank you for trusting me," he murmured, kissing me again, his tongue lashing against mine.

Then he slowly started to thrust into me, stretching me further. I moaned lowly, burying my face into his neck and wrapping the leg he wasn't holding around his waist. His hands went to my hips, allowing me to wrap both my legs around his waist. He grasped my hips tightly, pressing me against the wall again as he thrust up into me, going harder. I moaned loudly, throwing my head back as he thrust hard, biting at the skin of my neck gently, sending shivers throughout my form.

"Ah…yes…harder, Yuuta!" I cried as he hit that spot inside me.

He grinned against my skin and pinned me against the wall, thrusting hard and steadily into that spot. Now that he'd found it, he was going to exploit it.

"You feel so good, little one. I…love you," he moaned against my pulse, thrusting hard again, starting to up the speed for me.

I jolted, a knot forming in my throat. I couldn't say it back. I didn't love him back. I wouldn't lie to him. Even if it hurt his feelings, I wasn't going to lie to him. He thrust hard, hitting that spot forcefully, eliciting another hot moan from my lips.

"Ah, yes…I'm close, Yuuta," I cried, moaning as his thrusts quickened again, trying to ignore the heartache in his eyes as he thrust into me fast and hard, hitting the spot each time without fail.

"Me too, Ivan…Come for me. Come, my little red fox," he groaned, grasping my cock and stroking in time with his thrusts, kissing me hotly and passionately.

Three more of his thrusts and strokes and I came with a cry, spilling across our chests, my body jerking as he thrust a couple of more times before coming. He filled me in a hot rush as I cried out over him, spasming and shuddering.

"Ah-ha…so hot…," I moaned, panting as he just held me gently against the wall, still planted firmly inside me.

"I understand. Your heart still belongs to the vampire. You're so sweet. But please, lie to me now, if just a little bit. If it doesn't hurt you too much, tell me you love me," he said, dropping his head onto my shoulder.

Unable to help it, I stroked his hair. If that's what he wanted, I could lie to him—just a little bit, like he said.

"Yuuta…I love you too," I said, kissing his neck as he pulled me back into the water with him, adjusting the taps so that it was warmer. "It's not completely a lie. I feel something for you. I care about you. It could be love. I just don't know. But it's something strong enough for me to want you like this. I just want to stay in your arms, to have the delicious feeling of you inside me. So I don't mind saying it," I murmured softly, lifting his face and kissing him sweetly.

"You are so wonderful, Ivan. How dare they hurt you as they have. Let me wash you, and then we can lie together until I have to leave for my mission," he said softly, holding me gently as the water ran over us.

"That sounds lovely," I murmured, kissing him softly as he retrieved the soap blindly.

# Chapter 9

# Turning the Tides

*Markus*

"Zarrack, we've been waiting far too long. We need to get to Ivan. I can't wait anymore," I growled at the Hunter, who sat jotting things down in a notebook at the little desk in the hotel room we shared.

"It's time. We're going in to get him out tonight. He should still be in the hospital. Once he's out and turned, we attack. When was the last time you fed? You'll need to be strong in case we get attacked," Zarrack said, tapping the pen against his lips before setting it down and pushing back from the desk.

"I haven't fed…in a while," I admitted ashamedly, rubbing the back of my neck.

The last time I had fed was in the ground healing, and that was on rodents.

"I thought so. Here. I'm not appalled by it. So go ahead and feed from me. It will make this mission manageable," he said, turning in the chair and offering me his wrist.

"Won't that make you weak?" I asked, not too keen on the idea of drinking from anyone but Ivan.

It was impractical and selfish, and I needed to be strong to save him.

"No. I'm strong from years of blood loss and abuse. I wasn't always a skilled Hunter," Zarrack said, unbuckling the leather strap around his neck.

My jaw dropped as he bared the skin there. It looked as if someone had ripped into his flesh like an animal.

"I used to be nothing more than a food source to a vile, unkind vampire. When I got…too old for his tastes, he ripped my throat out. I was saved by a Hunter that was coming to eliminate said vampire. He was the one that taught me not all vampires are evil beasts. I'm not comfortable letting you at my neck, but that's because the skin is sensitive. So stop stalling—Ivan told me how good you are at that—and just feed. We're wasting time," he explained, replacing the collar and holding his arm out to me.

I nodded, carefully grasping his arm as my fangs slowly slid into view.

"Thank you for your sacrifice," I murmured softly as I leaned over and carefully sank my fangs into the beating pulse of his inner arm, the crease of the elbow where it hurt less and wouldn't become aggravated by sword fighting.

My words were ones I had been taught as a young vampire, to honor those you fed from. They seemed to ease Zarrack, who had been tense without my realizing. He knew what they meant. He had to. He said he studied the slayers' histories, so he had to have known the words spoken by the sect of vampires that had once served side by side with the Hunters.

The first gulp of his blood seared my tongue, hot and tangy with the sharp taste of metal, slayer blood through and through. But it was good and quenching nonetheless. I drew back after several swallows, shuddering softly as my strength doubled, if not tripled. Refreshed by the strong blood, I looked up at Zarrack and found him watching me, a pang in his eyes as I drew away. I couldn't seem to decipher the look. It wasn't one of lust but perhaps longing. I sighed and stood, rolling my shoulders. With my strength renewed, I could rescue Ivan. I could fix this fucked-up mess, and we could go on with our lives. I would make Ivan a vampire, give him the immortality he craved, and keep him at my side forever.

*Ivan*

I lay naked in Yuuta's bed, awaiting his return from his mission. It was a regular occurrence for us. I would be waiting in his bed for him, ready for kisses and cuddles. Now it was different. With him no longer afraid to fill me, I could probably convince him into a deliciously passionate night. He deserved it after all he had done for me. When the door slammed open, I didn't expect to see Markus there, with Zarrack at his back. I felt my throat close up, cutting off my breath as I yanked the covers around my body, something I had never done around Markus.

"W-What are you doing here? They want to kill you! Are you out of your mind, Zarrack, bringing him here like this?" I exclaimed, wondering if I should feel guilty for him finding me in another man's bed.

But I didn't feel that way at all. I was surviving. I was trying to be happy with what I had left. Before Markus could respond, I felt a pain tear through my chest and coughed hard, the action making blood spill from my mouth.

"Oh God! Zarrack, what's wrong? What's happening to him?" Markus shouted, rushing to the bed and pulling me into his arms.

I struggled, pushing against his chest as I coughed harder, more blood spilling from my lips. My head was spinning, my ears ringing as my body collapsed against the bloodied sheets, blood spilling out of my mouth and nose. Was this the end? Truly this time? Or was I just being made to suffer more?

"Something in his stomach must have torn, weakened by his failing liver. He's dying...I don't think there is a way...to save him...," Zarrack choked out, taking my hand in his, squeezing it.

"H-Hey, buddy, don't cry for me. At least, I won't be in pain anymore," I said weakly before coughing up more blood, clutching his hand with the little strength I had.

"Hold on, little buddy. I'm here for you. Markus...could... could you turn him? Would that...would that save him?" Zarrack asked desperately, tears tracking his face.

He truly was my friend; he cared. Too bad I had to be dying to truly see it.

"S-Save…your breath…He won't turn me…doesn't want me…to become a monster," I gasped out, feeling as though I couldn't breathe, the agony in my chest flaring out through my whole body.

"Markus, remember what I told you. Not all vampires are bad. You're not, so Ivan won't be either. Just…save him," Zarrack said to Markus, who sat sobbing beside us, crimson tears tracking down his cheeks.

"I'll do it, Ivan. I can't lose you again. I've realized that, and if making you like me will save you, I will do it!" he exclaimed, pulling my limp and weak body into his arms and burying his fangs hurriedly into my neck.

My vision quickly wavered and went black, leaving me to wonder if we'd been too late.

*Yuuta*

I sighed, exhausted after my mission, a particularly rough one at that. I took my coat off and draped it over my shoulder, heading toward my room, when I was hit with the powerful stench of blood. My eyes widened as I launched toward my room, hoping to all hell that Ivan was okay. I slammed through the door and found a still, lifeless-looking Ivan laid out on bloodstained sheets, a vampire straddling him as Zarrack helped the fanged bastard slice his own wrist and press it to Ivan's parted lips. A roar of rage ripped from my chest, and I threw myself at the vampire, knocking him off the edge of the bed and falling with him in a tangle of limbs. He looked more shocked than monstrous as he seemed to try to struggle to get up to return to his defilement of Ivan, determined.

"No! You don't understand! He's dying! This is the only way to save him!" the vampire cried, still struggling to get free.

I felt a sharp pang in the back of my head, and my world swam as I unwillingly loosened my grasp. Zarrack stood over me with the remnants of my lamp in hand, looking apologetic.

"Sorry, Yuuta, but I can't let Ivan die. You'll understand soon. We'll explain it to you. But for now, go night-night," Zarrack said, punching me in the jaw and knocking me unconscious.

*Markus*

"I'm sorry. I know he is your friend. You shouldn't have had to do that," I told Zarrack, who still stood over the other Hunter's unconscious form.

"He's not my friend, never was. I don't understand this. This is his room. Yuuta's room. Why was Ivan here? Why was he willingly naked in his bed and completely unharmed? I'm missing something here," the young Hunter said, looking at Ivan, then back down at the Hunter Yuuta.

"I…I don't know…but his scent is all over Ivan. It's permeating his body. Could they be lovers? Or was Ivy manipulating him to keep himself safe?" I asked, still feeding Ivan blood as it started to change him, his body almost rebooting in a sense.

Just a little more and he'd be on his own.

"I don't know, Markus. But I trust Ivan. He is a good man struggling to survive. You read his file, what they did to him. He has his reasons, I'm sure," Zarrack said, coming back to the bed and sitting beside us as I drew my wrist away from Ivan's lips.

He had started to respond to it, his mouth pulling at the wound. But he'd had enough to turn, and I was feeling light-headed. Zarrack's arms came around me from behind, and he pressed his unmarked arm against my mouth.

"You're feeling weak again, I can tell. Here," he said softly, his skin feeling hot against my lips.

I frowned, suddenly feeling like I was indulging an alcoholic with his favorite wine. But I needed it. However selfish it was, I would give in to it for now. I grasped his arm and bit down carefully, taking the first draw of hot metallic Hunter blood. It was powerful stuff, but nothing could replace Ivan's. I drew back after a few moments, licking the wound kindly as I did.

"Thank you, Zarrack. But don't do that again. It's bad for you," I said, concerned for him.

He nodded at me softly, sitting back.

"How long until the change is complete? I've never seen it done before," he asked softly, brushing a lock of hair out of Ivan's face and glancing back at Yuuta to make sure he was still unconscious.

He hadn't moved and was still out. Good. Hopefully he'd stay that way until Ivan woke up again.

*Yuuta*

I felt my consciousness slowly return but stayed still, feigning it. They were still in the room, and I couldn't take both of them at once. I was strong, but they were stronger as a team. I stayed quiet, listening to their conversation.

"I hope he can forgive me when he wakes up. I should have just agreed to turn him before it got this bad. I was wrong. I couldn't handle losing him. A lifetime with him wasn't ever going to be enough," the vampire said softly, his voice gravelly with tears.

"He will, Markus. I'm sure. You were all he talked about," Zarrack responded.

The vampire's name was Markus? Ivan's Markus?

"I hope so. This Yuuta fellow…can we trust him? What was he doing with Ivan?" Markus asked, the mattress shifting some as the two moved around.

"I don't know what happened while I was gone, but I know that Ivan was his favorite toy. It's no doubt that he probably bribed his way into keeping him for himself. Ivan was probably manipulating him to survive. He was good at that. He told me it's how he keeps them from hurting him as bad," Zarrack's voice said.

I fought the urge to frown; my Ivan wasn't manipulating me. He'd willingly come to my bed. He used manipulation to keep from being harmed. That made sense. He was smart. He'd told me all that he had suffered before coming to me and had told me what the Weres had done to him. It made me feel so sick, thinking that those who were supposed to be our allies had done that to a human whose only sin was loving a vampire. He was so kind and had endured so much at *our* hands. No wonder he hung with a vampire and avoided us. Maybe we weren't the good guys after all.

"I don't know. But it better not be that, or I'm…I'll kill him?" Markus said, sounding angry but also so unsure of performing that action.

He was a vampire. He should be accustomed to killing. That's what they did, didn't they?

"*I'll* kill him if that's the case. I left him safe, and my word and money meant nothing to keep him that way. I screwed up and left him vulnerable. I shouldn't have left him here," Zarrack said, anger in his own voice, the bed shifting again as someone stood up off the bed.

"His heartbeat is faster, like he's awake. Open your eyes, eavesdropper, and explain yourself, or I will feed you to him when he wakes," Markus's voice said from right next to me.

My eyes shot open, and I found him crouching over me. I jolted away from him, glaring at him.

"Back off, fang face. You left him. You hurt him. He came to me. We're lovers now. He will never forgive you! He died for you, and you still left him! I love him, and…he loves me!" I shouted at him, half lying as I shoved him away from me.

He fell back on his ass, and Zarrack leapt off the bed and landed evenly at his side. But my eyes were on Markus, my words having the desired effect on him. He was shocked then, wearing an expression of deep agony.

"And how will you feel when he wakes up as a vampire? Will you still love him when he needs your blood to sustain himself?" Markus asked me harshly.

I had already thought of that and had accepted that. I loved him, and I could keep him from being evil. I would keep protecting him.

"I will do it for him. I told you I love him. I would never hurt him! Not even now!" I growled, getting up and shoving past Zarrack so I could go to Ivan's side, stroking his face. "I should have skipped the mission and stayed with him. We knew his days were numbered.

I should have spent every second of it with him. If you hadn't come, he'd be gone. I'd have come home to him, cold in *our* bed," I said, choking up as I accidentally put my hand in the blood that soaked the sheets.

I heard a snarl from behind me, a jealous snarl, and felt myself smirk through my tears.

*Markus*

I tried to launch at the bastard touching *my* Ivan and snarled, hating him, but, at the same time, so happy that someone had been able to love Ivan when I couldn't. I looked at him, his face covered in tears as he pulled Ivan into his arms.

"We need him on our side. You can't kill him," Zarrack whispered, holding me back from attacking him.

"Fine," I whispered and turned to Yuuta, feeling exhausted. "He will need blood when he wakes. Zarrack's donated twice already, and I'm not human. Are you truly willing to help him?" I asked, testing him and hoping, in the end, Ivan would forgive and choose me.

He looked up at me, face going deeply serious.

"I would give him anything and everything he needs," he said, his expression one of deep devotion.

I swallowed back my jealousy and rage for the time being and nodded. I had to make a few more sacrifices for Ivan's wellbeing. I could do that.

"Then I will accept your presence for now because he will need you in these first few weeks after the change," I said, gritting my teeth and climbing up on the bed beside him.

I let him continue to hold Ivan and just took Ivan's hand in mine. Yuuta caught my gaze and nodded. Together we would wait.

*Ivan*

It seemed I was doing a lot of waking up with a foggy memory. It was just an expectation at this point. My first perception was that I was in someone's arms and that they smelled really good. But not perfume good. More like, food good—savory with a pinch of spice. The next thing that came to my attention was that my skin was sticky, and I felt as if I'd been coated in something. I couldn't put my finger on it.

"He's waking up," a voice whispered nearby.

It was so familiar, but I couldn't place it either. I finally remembered how to open my eyelids, and my eyes caught movement in front of me. I slowly focused on the face and managed a smile.

"Zarrack? What happened? I feel funny. Was I drugged?" I asked, my words coming out slowly but clearly with no slurring or stuttering.

"Hey, buddy. It's okay. You were dying, and now you're a vampire. You're not thinking straight because you need blood. Yuuta's gonna help you with that. Is that okay? He's right behind you, and he says it's okay," Zarrack said, smiling carefully, standing at the edge of the bed and talking to me as if I were a child.

I frowned and turned, my joints almost feeling rusty. Yuuta sat behind me, lounging on our pillows, his long sweeping hair bound back.

"It's all right, little one. Come on and drink up so you can be strong," Yuuta murmured gently.

My heart soared. This must be some sort of dream, a fever dream that was impossible. But my body was moving without my instruction as he carefully nicked his neck with the pin from his uniform, a bubble of blood forming there. I licked my lips and leaned against him, the savory scent growing stronger.

"That's it, Ivan. But remember to be gentle. You don't want to hurt him. You love each other," Zarrack's voice said from behind me.

It registered, giving me more control over my body. I nodded my agreement, feeling the sharp, albeit dainty, fangs in my mouth.

"I'm not worried you'll hurt me. Just hurry, hot brand. You need it because you are brand new," Yuuta said worriedly.

I nodded again, leaning in and lapping at the dot of blood from the pinprick. He groaned and wrapped his arms around me, pulling my body tight to his own. I licked the spot again, nuzzling against it softly.

"I think I love you," I whispered and carefully, unsurely bit down over his calm pulse, eyes sliding closed as the first gush of his blood hit my tongue.

It was so hot and tangy, like a steak wonderfully spiced and gravied. But it was blood, not food—human food anyway. I was clearly a vampire in this dream. So it was food to me, and it was amazing. I wrapped my arms around his shoulders and ground against his crotch, feeling a surge of lust as he moaned beneath me. I drew back, panting and blushing, my body betraying my arousal. The drop of blood that rolled down my chin from the corner of my mouth was captured by Yuuta's thumb as he followed the trail up, then pressed his thumb into my mouth. Lust showed in his eyes, love nipping at its heels, and I happily suckled at his thumb, smiling around it.

"That's enough," I heard a voice that made my body go cold as I turned toward it.

Markus sat in the chair in the corner of the room away from us. My heart sank. This dream was turning into a nightmare as he stood and stalked over, grabbing Yuuta's wrist. He yanked *my* Yuuta away from me, his thumb getting nicked by my fangs as it was forcefully removed from my mouth.

"Markus, stop it. This is *my* dream. You left me to die and no longer have a right to decide. In this dream, I want Yuuta. This is a weird dream. But I'm glad it is…because I could never choose between you two, especially after you hurt me. This is probably a fever dream as I recall dying. So perhaps this is so I can get one last moment with at least one of you. Fate has been so cruel it's enough to wish I wasn't born. I seem to be the root of everyone's pain," I said, no longer excited as I looked down at my hands, feeling the weight of my words before I felt the tears on my face. I lifted a hand to touch them and came away with watered-down blood. "In the end…*I* am the monster," I said, laughing painfully and resting my head on my knees.

"This isn't a dream, Ivan. You're a vampire now. I turned you. The emotions you're feeling are elevated because you are a fledgling. Your body is adjusting and leaves your natural mental state off-balance. Lust and hunger will be the predominant feelings as you slowly finish the physical part of the change," Markus explained.

I frowned deeply.

"Then I'll just have to deny the lust. I don't…want to hurt either of you, and I can't choose between you two now. I love you both so deeply, for your kindness and your worry, for your thoughtfulness, for the feel of you inside me. I could not have only one of you in my life. So I will deny lust and hunger if I have to. I can't choose," I said, feeling like I had a knife in my chest, bloodied tears pouring down my face.

Yuuta moved, cupping my face and making me look at him.

"You don't have to choose. You can take my blood. Use me as I once used you. I will forfeit my hold on you because I can't see you in pain like this. He's better for you now anyway. He'll know how to take care of you, teach you how to be a good, strong vampire. I'll give you what you need, and you can forget about me. Let any love you have for me fade. I didn't deserve you. I took advantage of you. I used you for my own selfish desires. You should hate me, not love me," Yuuta said, twisting the metaphorical knife in my chest.

My tears flowed heavier as my already-destroyed world continued to crumble around me.

"No, I can't do that to you. I can share you. I can't see you hurting like this. It's my fault that you even needed a reason to fall in love with someone else. I can suffer the consequences of it. He loves you greatly, so much so that he was willing to give you up to make you happy," Markus said, more pain there in his eyes now.

Either way, it hurt them. *I* was still the cause. What was wrong with me?

"I can live with that," Yuuta said, nodding softly at me and caressing my cheek.

"E-Either way, I hurt you both…I'm the monster," I choked out, looking at them, wanting to be held; but all I could do was wrap my arms around myself.

Yuuta jolted toward me and wrapped his arms around me tightly, petting my hair that was hard and crinkly with dried blood.

"No, no, no. You are not a monster. You're my beautiful little hot brand. We just both love you so much the idea of sharing you is painful. We're like children fighting over the same delicious treat. There is plenty enough for both of us, but our pride makes us selfish. We'll make it work. We'll do it for you because we love you," he said, stroking my hair despite the fact that it felt so horrendous with the blood dried in it.

"Yes…Well said, Yuuta," Markus murmured, wrapping his arms around us, kissing my shoulders.

"All right, boys, let him up. I'm thinking he would like to shower," Zarrack's voice broke through the touching moment.

But he was right. It felt nice in their arms, but my body felt gross and sticky. My hair was a crunchy mess for sure.

"He's right. I feel gross. Let me go clean up, and then I will happily let you hold me," I said with a soft laugh.

Both Markus and Yuuta laughed with me, both placing a soft kiss on either one of my cheeks as they let me go, smiling at me.

"We'll clean up here while you wash. That way, you'll have a good place to rest and catch up together," Zarrack said, helping me off the bed and urging me toward the bathroom.

I laughed softly and swatted at him, slipping into the bathroom and shutting the door between him and me. I started the taps, having flashes of me and Yuuta's first time as a couple in the shower. I smiled, shivering softly from the memory as I stepped into the warm water, watching the blood get swept away in pink riverlets down the drain. It actually hit me then. I was a vampire now. No more almost dying. No more humanity… No more Miriam. No more Danny. I felt a sob surge up in my chest, and I covered my mouth as the sound croaked out of me. What was happening to my world? It was crumbling with every step I took.

*Yuuta*

"Is it wise to stay here? Perhaps we should move back to Ivan's house. Hiding in plain sight here isn't the best idea. A Hunter harboring two vampires won't go over well if we're discovered," Markus said softly, picking up the pieces of the smashed lamp up out of the rug.

His eyes pried over the carpet, easily locating every last shard.

"He might be right, Zarrack. Our best course of action would be to weapon up and escape now while the alarm is low. We've been going under the radar as of recently, but who's to say we won't be noticed at any moment," I said, agreeing with Markus, as I peeled the bloodied sheets of the bed with a thick *shick* sound.

It had soaked into the mattress and thoroughly ruined it. I stuffed the sheets into a garbage bag. There was no saving them either.

"That could work. The alarm isn't that low, though. I may have broken into the confidential room and stolen some files. But anyways, I was the only one that found Ivan's address when I was sent to bring him in. It was my mission and should be filed in my report. We could steal it too and destroy it. It's not like he's a public figure. He wasn't easy to locate to begin with," Zarrack said gently, taking the cases off of my pillows.

They were only spattered with blood, not enough to soak through luckily.

"Then it's decided. Once we're all cleaned up, Yuuta, pack your valuables. I can make a quick burn bomb. I don't wanna leave Ivan's blood on the mattress for them to find. Call me careful, but I didn't live this long as a vampire being reckless," Markus said, tossing the fragments of lamp in the garbage bag with the sheets. I just couldn't understand why he kept out the electrical bits of the lamp.

"You're going to start a fire…in my room?" I exclaimed, startled by his words.

He nodded and opened my closet, digging around in it.

*Just make yourself at home, geez,* I thought to myself.

But I could see he was just being methodical. I didn't know how old he was, but the fact that he was an older vampire still alive today was a miracle in and of itself.

"Yes. Zarrack, can you check on Ivan? He's been in the bathroom for a long time," Markus replied.

Zarrack nodded. He was sending the only man that wasn't his lover. Smart. If he was having an emotional breakdown, either one of us would be the last one he'd wanna see. I sighed and went to his side in the closet. I would make nice. He was really trying for Ivan, so I would too, even if he wanted to burn my room down.

*Zarrack*

I knocked on the bathroom door, waiting for a response. When he didn't answer, I slowly cracked open the door, ignoring the smack of steam that poured out as I stepped into the room.

"Hey, buddy...are you doing okay?" I asked, spotting him curled into a ball in the bottom of the shower.

"No...," he said, voice sounding hollow.

I frowned, taking off my shirt and pants so I was in my boxers only. He needed a friend, but I would need my clothes dry for our escape. I set them aside and stepped into the shower, kneeling beside him.

"Talk to me. Tell me what's wrong. You know I'll always be here for you," I said, stroking his hair.

He'd washed it thoroughly, the blood gone so his hair lay smoothly on his skin.

"I just realized I may never get to see Miriam and Danny again. I can't...I'm a vampire now...No doubt I'll have to leave my life behind," he said, trembling where he lay.

I frowned and grasped his shoulders, yanking him up into my lap and hugging him.

"Listen, I will make sure that doesn't happen. They are your family. You will not lose them simply because you chose to *live*," I told him, making him look at me, my expression one of seriousness and determination.

He looked at me, eyes wide as he realized I was nearly as naked as he was, and he choked on a laugh.

"You really are pin straight and damn comfortable with it!" he said, laughing again.

I knew my words had soothed him, but come on. It wasn't that damn funny.

"Damn right. Now come on. You're wasting water. The other two are gonna want warm showers," I responded, playfully shoving him out of my lap and shaking my head as he let out another soft laugh.

The people I tie myself to. Damn.

# Chapter 10

# Cool Guys Don't Look
# at Explosions

*Ivan*

I sat in the chair, watching Markus work on something beside the bed with the innards of the smashed lamp and a couple bottles of chemicals. I had yet to have been told what they were doing, but whatever it was had Zarrack's interest as he watched closely.

"Oh, so you put that wire there and that one there. I see. But what causes the ignition?" he questioned, moving around the bed to look at it from another angle.

Yuuta crossed his arms, looking miffed. On his back, he had a backpack that he'd packed full of things from his room as I'd watched, delighted that he was staying with us; but it also meant that we were leaving. It must have been something they discussed whilst I was showering.

"We'll plug the lamp in, obviously. Electrical fires aren't hard to put out, but this will cause the chemicals to spread and explode. These chemicals are flammable and float on water. It's like combining electrical and grease fires together. It should keep them distracted long enough for us to get out of here," Markus explained.

I blinked. He sure knew a lot on the matter. He seemed to notice my stare and smiled.

"I daylighted as a firefighter a decade or two ago. Gave me a lot of useful knowledge in the matters of arson," he explained easily, seeming to finish what he was doing, and gestured for everyone to go toward the door.

"All right, once this triggers, we're gonna wanna book it. No stopping to watch because no doubt this will catch a lot of attention the minute it booms," Zarrack said, easing out the door, keeping it most of the way shut to hide that Markus was there.

The last thing we needed was for a nosy passerby raising the alarm on us. Yuuta followed after him, and I stood, walking toward the door. Yuuta's hand reached in and caught my wrist, pulling me out and shutting the door. The lights suddenly flickered, and Markus launched out the door and yanked it closed behind him just as the setup let out a hiss and exploded. It was a big enough explosion to make the heavy door shake.

"Let's go!" he exclaimed as I stalled, shocked by the flames already licking under the door.

I turned and realized that Yuuta and Zarrack were already down the hall and turning a corner. I nodded and took off, startled at the new speed with which I could move. Markus was right at my side, looking at me proudly. I quirked an eyebrow in confusion, unsure what he was proud of. I filed the thought away and kept moving, catching up to Yuuta and Zarrack easily just as alarms started to blare.

"This way!" Yuuta shouted, kicking the glass out of the main hall window.

It was a large bay-style window and shattered easily. You'd think the Hunters would have thicker glass for safety but apparently not. I felt my heart squeeze when Yuuta jumped up on the windowsill and fell forward into empty air.

"What are you doing! This is the fourth floor!" I exclaimed, stepping closer and watching him free-fall, shifting in the air at the last moment so he landed on one palm and flipped himself to his feet.

"Just jump! You'll be fine!" Zarrack replied, running and leaping out the window with a laugh. "Silly vampire, afraid of heights!"

I heard him shout from the air as he did a somersault and landed on one knee.

"Crazy-ass Hunters. Looks like it's my turn. I hate heights," Markus muttered, shaking his head as he climbed the sill like Yuuta had and leapt, his coat whipping around him as the air blew past him.

He landed in a roll that cooled his momentum. I swallowed. I could do this. Couldn't be that hard. They made it look so easy.

I decided on the running start like Zarrack had, taking a deep breath and jolting forward. Forgetting about the new speed I possessed, I miscalculated the distance, and my ankles hit the sill before I managed the jump. I flopped out the window instead of jumping or free falling and felt myself turning and twisting in the air as I tried to get my bearings. I landed on my back on the hot pavement, grateful for the clothes Zarrack had let me borrow. Being bare ass on hot pavement was not on the top of my bucket list, that was for sure. Once my ears stopped ringing, I sat up slowly, finding the three successful daredevils standing behind me. Zarrack was clearly holding back a snicker while Yuuta looked concerned. Markus just sighed, holding his hand out to help me up, pulling me against his chest and kissing me softly.

"Well, at least my little klutz is sturdier," he said gently, making me blush softly.

"All right, horn balls. Control the urges until we're in a safer location, yeah?" Zarrack said, gesturing toward a sleek black motorcycle. "I'll take Ivan with me. Markus can ride with you," he said to Yuuta, who frowned.

"I don't have a car, and my bike's in the shop…," he protested.

Zarrack rolled his eyes.

"I thought of that. That's why I stole the keys to…I think it's Lukai's bike. So take that one, and let's move it," he replied, tossing Yuuta a set of keys.

He caught it, and a vengeful smirk spilled across his lips.

"Happily. Come on, Markus," Yuuta said as he started off toward another bike farther down the line.

I knew he liked the idea of taking the bastard's motorcycle and probably planned to destroy it when he no longer needed it. Guess he wasn't done torturing him.

It was late when we made it back to my house. I could feel the exhaustion like a weight on my shoulders and stumbled as I climbed off the motorcycle. I was instantly swept up into someone's arms and realized that it was only Zarrack. In fact, we had seemed to have lost Yuuta and Markus back on the highway.

"They'll be here in a bit. I know about as much as you do. But you should know by now that we can trust them. Let's get you fed and in bed. You're clearly exhausted," he murmured and carried me up the steps onto the porch, shifting me enough to open the door.

The setting sun gave us just enough light as he carried me down the hall and up the stairs.

"My door is the last one on the right," I murmured when he paused on the landing, likely wondering which was mine. There were a lot of rooms on this floor after all.

"I was just balking at the sheer size of your home. I forget you're a rich boy. You just don't act like it," he said, continuing down the hall and getting the door opened.

"My uncle and father built this house. We didn't buy it. My parents had hoped to have a large family. It just didn't work out that way." He paused in the doorway, looking over the master bedroom with wide eyes.

*Balking again, Zarrack?* I thought.

I'd have to give him a tour in the morning when we got up.

He carried on into the bedroom, smiling kindly as he gently laid me in my bed. The sheets were neatly made, which was funny because I hadn't made it before I had left with him what felt like years ago. Markus must have been staying in my bed and had dutifully made it. It brought a smile to my lips as I rolled over, pulling the comforter over my body, burying my face in the pillow, and catching his sweet scent clinging to it. Then Zarrack pressed his wrist under my nose, crouching beside the bed.

"You need to feed first. New vamps need a lot of blood to keep moving," he said softly, seeming very knowledgeable in the subject.

I shook my head tiredly, pushing his arm away.

"I'll just wait for Markus and Yuuta," I said.

He frowned but nodded, respecting my wishes without pushing the issue.

"Fine. But if you wake up needing it before they get here, I'll be downstairs," he said softly, tucking the blanket along my side.

"There are four guest rooms. You needn't sleep on the couch," I said, yawning softly.

He nodded and stood walking to the door. I was asleep before the door clicked shut behind him. I, for once, did not dream.

*Yuuta*

I took an exit off the highway, a random one with no real destination. I just knew I wanted a moment away from everyone and everything else. I needed to talk to Markus and get things figured out before I returned with him to Ivan's side. I heard Markus try to yell at me; but I ignored him, falling into the hum of the motorcycle's engine until I pulled over in a remote, nearly empty parking lot. I cut the engine and waited for him to get off. When he reluctantly did so, I swung my leg off the bike and stood. I turned to him, seeing his questioning expression.

"What are we doing here, Yuuta? We lost Ivan and Zarrack," he asked me, frowning some.

"We need to discuss how this is going to work. The three of us. What are the rules and boundaries?" I said, crossing my arms and taking my usual stance.

Zarrack called it my "badassery" pose. Markus looked at me and nodded softly.

"You're right. I'm a top through and through. I can't give in on that. But anything else, I will do for you and him. You're...not a bad-looking man. It wouldn't appall me to kiss you or touch you." he said, blushing faintly as he spoke.

I nodded, blushing softly myself. It was good that we could talk through this like adults.

"I'm a top too. But I wouldn't be appalled by it either. I wouldn't mind you feeding off me either. I thought I despised vampires, thought they were all evil. But I was very wrong. You two aren't evil. You're good and honorable," I admitted, smiling gently.

He moved closer, still blushing.

"Let's try a kiss now then. I really want this to work," he said.

I let him pull me against him by my hips, his fingers looping in my belt loops. I swallowed and nodded, wrapping my arms around his shoulders hesitantly. He leaned in; and I met him in the middle, our lips touching softly, a small chaste kiss that deepened slowly. He nipped at my lip gently, and I parted them for his seeking tongue. Our tongues danced slowly, my tongue flicking against his fangs, darting slightly against the roof of his mouth. Finally he drew back, both of us panting softly from the wonderful kiss.

"That was actually rather good," I murmured, smiling softly.

He nodded, smiling at me gently.

"This will work. Now let's go. I have a feeling that Ivan won't feed off of Zarrack. He'll be able to see what I see in him. It concerns me that he has such an addiction," he murmured softly as I got back on the bike.

"Addiction? What addiction?" I asked, frowning deeply as he spoke, joining me on the bike again.

"You know he used to be a not-so-good vampire's food source, right? Well, the bite can cause an addiction over time. He's got it. I didn't realize it at first. It hit me the second time…He's like an addict that had his first taste of his drug of choice in a long time. Ivan's sharper than I. He'd catch it sooner because he doesn't want to hurt Zarrack, wouldn't want to worsen his addiction," he explained to me, wrapping his arms around my waist this time, opposed to holding onto the seat.

It felt kinda nice honestly, to have his warm arms around me, my lips still tingling from his kiss. This would work. I would have a family of my own that wasn't just pity guardians, raising me amongst the Hunters.

I started the motorcycle and felt his grip tighten slightly as I drove the bike in the direction that would take us home. Feeling him rest his head on my shoulder, I relaxed and finished the trip toward the house. It was a quick drive, and I pulled up to the dark house. The only lights were the porch and what looked like the living room light. I turned off the bike and got off, hesitantly taking Markus's hand. He looked at me with a softly surprised expression, but his lips split into a soft smile.

"Come on. I'm sure Ivan's starving. He's new, so he needs quite a bit of blood right now, right?" I asked gently.

He nodded, squeezing my hand softly.

"Right, he really needs you right now," Markus murmured.

I cupped his cheek, laying a fleeting kiss on his soft lips.

"He needs both of us," I said, making him smile some more as I pulled him toward the house—toward our family.

*Ivan*

"Ivan, little one, time to wake up and feed. We're home," a voice murmured gently as I felt someone shake me gently.

I slowly cracked my eyes open, blinking until I could focus on the face in front of me. Yuuta had knelt down by the bed, smiling gently at me. I smiled back sleepily, yawning widely.

"That's it. Wake up, Ivy. You need to feed. Then we can go to sleep together. Does that sound nice? The three of us all cuddled together," Markus's voice came from behind me, lips pressing against my clothed shoulder.

"That sounds wonderful…Mmph…Yuuta…" I felt myself purr softly as he slid up onto the bed beside me, helping me sit up.

"Do you need help this time, or are you hungry enough to bring out your fangs on your own?" he asked, stroking my cheek.

My tongue lashed against my teeth, finding my fangs had already slid into place, sharp and ready.

"They're already out. I don't need help this time," I murmured gently, feeling him slide his fingers into my hair, gently pulling my head flush to his neck.

I blushed softly, tonguing the smooth pulse in his neck that jumped with excitement as my tongue ran along it.

"Mm…are you trying to excite me, hot brand? Just bite already," he growled softly, fingers tightening almost painfully in my hair.

I didn't need any more urging as my stomach rumbled hungrily. I groaned softly, biting down hard and fast, the action pulling a gasp from his mouth. His fingers released my hair; and his hands went around my waist, holding me gently as I sucked in the first mouthful—the tangy, delicious fluid coating my tongue and rolling down my throat with ease, just the slightest edge of metallic. My mouth stayed flush to his skin as he rolled us, so I lay with my back against the bed, his body over mine. It was all warmth and excitement, my tiredness gone as I felt my lust ignite to life.

"Yuuta, I don't think he's quite so tired anymore," I heard Markus's voice murmur as I drew back from Yuuta's neck, lapping the wound more than necessary.

It elicited a lusty groan from Yuuta's throat as he pushed himself up so he was no longer leaning his full weight on me.

"No, I don't think he is either. Think you've got enough energy to help me satisfy our little one?" Yuuta asked, turning to smirk at my other beloved.

I blinked, noticing something different about their relationship, but my lust burned far too hot right now for me to put my finger on it.

"You know it. Let's see what he thinks of this," Markus murmured, grasping Yuuta's chin and kissing him deeply while he was still suspended over me.

I blinked and groaned, the sight making my cock jerk in my borrowed pants.

"Oh God! This *must* be a dream. There is no way something this hot is real," I moaned as Markus drew back from the heated kiss.

"It isn't a dream, Ivy. We've come to an agreement of sorts. Now strip so we can help to satisfy those annoying fledgling urges. We'll always be here to help you," Markus murmured softly, eyes locked with mine as Yuuta moved to sit at his side.

I blushed deeply, my heart aching with the amount of happiness it was trying to contain.

I sat up, feeling their eyes on me as I moved. I slowly slid my hands down my sides, locating the hem of the solid-black sleeveless shirt I wore. It really wasn't my style anyway. I slowly slid it up my body, baring my skin an inch at a time, still feeling their gazes like searing fingers on the bared flesh. It made me self-conscious, remembering the ragged scars that marred my skin.

"So beautiful," I heard Yuuta murmur, his usual statement when I stripped for him.

It made my anxiety fade and made me blush ever deeper as I pulled the shirt off the last few inches and tossed it off the bed. I got up on my knees, wobbling and unbalanced as I carefully unbuttoned the borrowed pants, which were several inches too long for me, the waist fitting perfect. It was always my short stature that threw off the look. I often just paid for specially tailored pants to get over the pain of mundane shopping, my one indulgence. But alas, I couldn't tailor borrowed pants.

I was suddenly knocked backward, the pants tugged off my body none too gently. I blinked rapidly and giggled at the impatient Markus, who yanked the pants from my feet and threw them to join the shirt on the floor.

"You were taking too long," Markus grumbled, leaning down and placing a kiss above my belly button, making my skin twitch and tremble.

My lust was hot enough to set the world ablaze, unhindered by my flushed cheek and mild embarrassment at having both of them in the bed at once. This certainly wasn't something I was accustomed to.

"I was enjoying the show. For an immortal with a lot of time, you sure are impatient," Yuuta teased.

Sometime during my stripping, he had lost his shirt and was unbuttoning his dark-colored jeans, his eyes on the two of us as if we were the best sight in the world.

"He is right, Markus. So impatient," I purred, feeling wetness on my chin before I even realized I was drooling just from watching Yuuta take his clothes off.

Yeah, I was definitely emotionally unstable right now. But that didn't seem like a bad thing anymore. I suddenly got an idea and grinned, hooking Markus's leg with my foot. It pitched him off-balance, and I pounced, straddling him before he could even focus on what I had done. This new speediness definitely took the cake.

"What are you doing, Ivy?" he asked, grinning up at me.

I smirked and grabbed either side of his button-up shirt. With a swift yank, I tore it from his body, the buttons flying and fabric tearing.

"That is for ruining one of my uniforms! Don't think I forgot that!" I said defiantly, knowing it was a daring move. But I was willing to face the consequences.

He made a face, then remembered and burst out laughing, grasping the back of my neck to yank me down for a hot kiss. There came a soft groan from beside us and glanced over at Yuuta, who'd removed his pants and returned to his seated position on the side of the bed. His cock twitched in excitement as he watched us, his lip bitten between his teeth. I grinned and reached out, gently grasping him in my hand. It forced a soft moan from his lips, and Markus grinned, seeming to get his own ideas.

"Ivy, you play with Yuuta. I'll be right back," he said gently, slipping out from underneath me and leaving the room.

I blinked, but knowing him, it could be anything. I simply turned to grin up at Yuuta who smiled back, the expression melting into a groan as I gave one quick stroke to the cock standing at attention in my hand.

"Mm…I believe I owe you a blow job or six," I said, grinning when my words caused his face to flush.

He opened his mouth, likely to protest, but I stopped him from speaking with a well-meaning flick of my tongue to the head of his cock. Before he could gather his thoughts, I slid a hand up his thigh to cup his balls gently. Whatever sentence he'd been forming cut off into a choked moan as my mouth engulfed the head of his cock, my hand massaging his balls gently.

"God, such a little hot brand," he groaned, fingers lacing in my hair as he gave up trying to protest my words.

*That's what I thought*, I muttered in my head as I slid my tongue around him, easing another few inches into my mouth.

My eyes slid closed as I lapped along him, moving slowly on purpose, the taste of him like manna on my tongue. Everything about this man was savory and wonderful I just couldn't get enough. He moaned, and I took the last several inches in one quick bob, nearly choking when he hit the back of my throat. It pulled a deep gasp from his mouth as I sucked hard, squeezing his balls lightly.

Just as I was really starting to get a good pace going—bobbing my head quickly as I worked his cock with lips, tongue, and teeth—my shoulders were grabbed; and I was yanked backward away from Yuuta. A disappointed whimper slipped from my lips, frowning at Markus that had me by my shoulders.

"All right, wrists," he demanded.

I blinked, holding up my wrists for him despite not knowing what exactly he wanted them for. All questions disappeared when he looped a rough rope around them, tying them together with a little bit of a lead to it. I quirked an eyebrow at him, then frowned as he yanked me forward and tied the extra rope to the bed frame, low and tight enough that I couldn't move out of my kneeling position.

"Normally I would have gone for silk rope or leather straps, but you have neither...So you'll have to deal with this until I can get us something more comfortable," he murmured, smirking softly and pulling a soft red bandana out of his pocket, folding it until it was a long flat rectangle.

"You didn't think to check the closet before the shed?" I piped up, pretending the rough rope didn't already have me on edge.

"Ooh, we're tying him up. Fun." Yuuta giggled, smiling.

It was the last thing I saw before the bandana was tied over my eyes, efficiently rendering me mostly blind.

"Now, as a vampire, your senses are already heightened, leaving every sound, sensation, taste as a new experience. When blinded, even temporarily, those experiences become something else altogether. You'll be a writhing mess long before we're done with you. How's that sound?" He asked, a hand running slowly down my side.

An involuntary shiver rolled through me, following the touch like a pleasant ripple.

"That...sounds wonderful," I said, biting my lip as my excitement rose further.

"Good. You're already tied up and blindfolded," he said with a snicker.

The bed shifted around me, and hands grasped my thighs and spread them so that I fell forward onto my chest, my arms stretched up above my head by the rope and my ass presented in the air like that of an animal in heat. A blush crept along my cheeks as the room fell silent but for the sounds of my lovers' movements and breathing. It made my heart race with excitement as I tried to locate who was where when I felt a hot tongue against the rim of my ass. I gasped lowly, my hands tightening into fists as the touch sent hot tingles of sensation throughout my lower half. The tongue swirled around the outside, but I was unable to wholly focus on the sensation as I was suddenly lifted and positioned on my elbows. There was a mouth suddenly on one of my nipples, suckling hotly, while fingers tweaked the other. I moaned and shuddered, my cock twitching, painfully hard.

"Ah...so good...too much...," I gasped out, shuddering as I had struggled to keep silent like they were so I could focus solely on the sensations and sounds alone.

Both men laughed, almost in sync, so I still couldn't tell who was who. Then the mouths were back on me, the tongue thrusting into my asshole as the mouth locked on my nipple again, teeth nipping at it as the fingers pinched suddenly. I moaned, unable to stop the sound from spilling from my mouth as I grew close from just these ministrations. Markus was right, the blindfold and inability to control my movements had left me a shuddering mess. The tongue withdrew from my asshole at the same time the mouth on my nipple switched to the other, making me jerk against the ropes and whimper.

There was movement again as whoever was behind me climbed down from the bed. I heard the footsteps move toward the nightstand and dig around in it. It had to be Markus. He knew I had lube in there. But then again, it was common sense that I would have it in there. I groaned, no closer to figuring out who was who than I had been before the blindfold went over my eyes. The bed moved as the person rejoined us on the bed. The sound of the bottle snapping open was a loud crack in the echoing silence of my bedroom. Then my body jolted as a slickened finger was pressed past the ring of muscle inside me, a moan that sounded as if it came from my toes slipped from my mouth. The lips teasing my nipples disappeared, and they were suddenly on mine, kissing me passionately. It was all the more hot and exciting while I could no longer tell who was who. Our tongues meshed, dancing hotly as he nipped mine. My breath sped as another finger was pressed inside me, the two lubed appendages scissoring suddenly, stretching me.

Suddenly both the fingers and the lips pulled back from me. But it was only momentarily as both men pressed their cocks to my skin in sync. I blushed fiercely, excitement making me shudder, as I eagerly opened my mouth to the heat pressed to my cheek, wiggling my ass lustily until someone's hands stilled my hips and I was suddenly filled to the hilt on both ends. Both men moaned above me, and it sent delighted shivers through my form. The two started to thrust, slowly and almost teasingly. I groaned in delight, the sound muffled by the hard cock thrusting between my lips. I suckled hard, tongue lapping along the underside eagerly. The thrusting quickened, falling out of sync as the two grunted and moaned. This was better than anything I'd ever felt before. I was in heaven as my body jerked and shuddered. I was now pretty sure that it was Markus in front of me and Yuuta behind me, but I didn't care. My mind went blank, and I let out a cry as I came across the sheets. Perhaps it was the vibration of my cry that pushed him over the edge, the cock in my mouth plunging as deeply as my mouth would allow and spilling down my throat. I gulped it down quickly, unable to swallow fast enough as a small drop slid down my chin. He pulled out of my mouth as the thrusts from behind became hard and faster, more moans spilling hotly from my lips as the blindfold was lifted up off my eyes. I panted softly as my vision was returned, my eyes meeting Markus's.

"That…was so…hot…," he panted and kissed me deeply as Yuuta let out a moan and thrust deep in me, cumming hotly inside me.

I spasmed between the two, shuddering in delight. He pulled out of me slowly, laying a delicate kiss along my spine.

"Fuck, little hot brand, sinful Mark. That was fantastic," Yuuta purred, collapsing beside me.

Markus blushed at the new nickname he had been given as he gently untied my wrists, kissing the marks it had made there before they healed as if they'd never been there at all. I grinned happily, efficiently worn out as the three of us got up and I shakily changed the sheets with their help. I didn't know about them, but I was certainly going to enjoy these fledgling urges up to the last ones.

# Chapter 11

# A Few Truths

*Zarrack*

I looked down at Ivan's cell phone in my hands. I hadn't yet returned it since our return home. Strange that I considered this place my home now, but it felt nice to simply be loved. None of the people here thought of me as a tool. I looked at the phone again and unlocked it, opening the text strand for his best friend, Miriam. Typing a quick message, I tried to set up a bit of a surprise for Ivan in order to lift his spirits. I wasn't going to fuck him like the other two. He wasn't my type, nor was he the right gender.

> Hey, hun! Ik it's late and all, but I wanted to let you know I was home from my vacay! Why don't you and Danny drop by for dinner tomorrow? I'll make your favorites!

I had texted and hoped it would be enough to coerce her into coming and bringing the boy. Then I could get their favorite stuff from Ivan and cook it myself. I promised he wouldn't lose them, and this was plan A.

The three had finally quieted down across the hall, and I rolled over on my side, plugging in the phone and setting it on the nightstand. I happily snuggled into the covers, relishing the softness of the bed and the pillows. Even for a guest bed, it was deliciously luxurious. Ivan didn't hold himself as a rich boy, but it definitely reflected in his beds and clothing. He was such a precious person, caring about everyone regardless of who they were or what they had done in their lifetime. I sighed and nuzzled down into the covers, suddenly so tired. I felt my eyes slip closed, yawning softly as I drifted off to sleep. It was going to be a long day tomorrow.

*Ivan*

I was jolted awake when something solid landed in the middle of my stomach, making me make a soft oomph sound. I sat up, picking up the object as I looked around the room, finding Zarrack standing at the end of the bed. The object in my hand was my cell phone vibrating with a phone call. I looked at the name flashing across the screen and blinked, answering it quickly.

"Uh...good morning, Miriam," I said, still half asleep as I quirked an eyebrow at Zarrack.

He simply smiled and put a finger to his lips. It was obvious he had sent a message and panicked when she called back instead.

"Hey, Ivan! I got your text this morning that you were home. Danny is ecstatic about dinner tonight. He missed you so much. We both did," Miriam replied, sounding tired despite her joyful conveyance of the message.

"Oh, I was so tired last night when I got home. I completely forgot I texted you! I can't wait to see you tonight. I will, of course, make your favorite!" I exclaimed cheerfully whilst glaring at Zarrack.

She laughed softly, and I frowned slightly, not liking that I sounded like a memory loss patient.

"You said that in the text, silly," she said with another laugh.

"Yeah, sorry. I was tired, and I just woke up after all. Jet lag is a bitch," I said, rubbing the back of my neck.

By now, Markus and Yuuta were awake and looking at each other in confusion.

"Aw, all righty, I'll let you go so you can wake up more and get your mind about you," she said softly.

There was shouting in the background, sounding like Danny.

"Danny says hi," she added with a giggle.

"Hey, Danny," I murmured gently and hung up, continuing my glare at Zarrack.

"What?" he asked innocently, smiling as if it was really no big deal.

"There are no groceries in the house…Now I have to go grocery shopping. You couldn't have waited a couple days?" I exclaimed, throwing a pillow at him that he effortlessly caught.

"No. I needed you to be reunited with your family. Just tell me what their favorites are, and I'll do all the work. You stay here and spend time with Markus and incidentally Yuuta. Just unwind and enjoy not being in danger for once. Yeah? Yeah. Now what will I be making?" he replied cockily, hands on his hips like a nagging housemaid.

I smirked; and Yuuta burst out laughing, sputtering something about Zarrack being a "mother hen," which got Markus laughing too. Poor Zarrack. I sighed softly and pinched the bridge of my nose.

"The two recipes stuck to the freezer with magnets. They're recipes that I edited until they were really good. Just follow my notes and you can't mess it up. You *can* follow instructions, right? You don't have to know how to cook so long as you follow the recipe to the T," I said, holding back my laugh as I teased him a bit myself.

He crossed his arms and scowled at me.

"I can cook *and* follow instructions. So it won't be a problem!" he exclaimed, sounding like he was declaring his place in a suicide mission.

Yuuta snickered and pretended to cough as he said, "Bullshit," making Markus and I both laugh again, smiling happily.

"All right, all right, no more picking. I know you can do it, Zarrack. I'm just joking," I murmured gently.

He nodded.

"Now, you three, relax. I can handle this," he said, smiling brightly and leaving.

Once he was gone, Markus piped up.

"You still have a fire extinguisher, right?" he asked.

I rolled my eyes at him.

"Yes...," I replied anyway, the three of us laughing together again.

"So what are we gonna do?" Yuuta asked, quirking an eyebrow at me.

I looked at him and slowly slid back underneath the blanket.

"Night," I said, closing my eyes and dropping my head on the pillow.

Markus laughed and flopped back down at my side, snuggling against me.

"My sentiment exactly. Sleep first," he murmured, burying his face against the back of my neck, his warm breath giving me goosebumps.

"How can you two still be tired? We had six hours of sleep!" Yuuta exclaimed.

I looked at him like he was crazy.

"Eight hours is the recommended amount of sleep necessary from a human. So you especially should be sleeping," Markus said, reaching an arm over me and yanking Yuuta down into the bed beside us.

I quickly curled around him so he couldn't get up easily. The man was strong, and I was small. If he really wanted to get up, he would have no problem doing so.

"Ugh, fine. But you owe me for making me sleep this much," he jokingly accused me.

"I'll think about it," I responded cheekily and closed my eyes again, feeling him move us closer so he and I were cuddled up to Markus.

I was glad at the ease with which the two had assimilated with each other. They seemed to have no problem sharing me and no issue with touching each other. It made my heart happy. I fell asleep in their arms with a delighted smile on my face. I felt wonderful and whole.

*Zarrack*

"Okay, grocery shopping like a normal human being. I can do this. Hope Ivan doesn't mind if I use his car. I will refill the gas if I remember," I muttered to myself as I looked over the recipes magnetted to the fridge, copying a list of the ingredients I would need for them as well as for some dessert.

With a sigh, I swiped Ivan's keys from the key hook and headed out the door. Climbing into the classic car felt like heaven as I started the engine and listened to the purr of it and dug through a stack of CDs.

"Three Days Grace, Linkin Park, Black Veil Brides. Man, do your tastes vary, Ivy," I muttered, picking a TDG album and popping it in the player, cranking the volume, and pulling down his driveway.

*Danny*

"I can't wait to see Daddy today, Mama," I said, lying on the floor in the living room of our apartment.

I had my favorite coloring book spread out in front of me with my crayons. They had been a present from "Uncle Ivan." Mama made me promise to call him that when we were with him. But he was actually my dad. He treated me like his son, so it really didn't matter to me. It made me so happy that he was always there for me without even knowing the truth.

"I know, baby. I'm hoping that the vacation was good for him. Maybe he's feeling better," Mama responded softly from the kitchen, doing the dishes from our breakfast.

"I think Uncle Markus will save him. He's special," I said, smiling as I colored in the vampire bat in the coloring book, making the little fangs red.

I had seen Uncle Markus be different. I had seen his fangs, and I knew that he would save my daddy. He loved him, so why wouldn't he? I hummed softly, knowing I'd confused Mama, but it would make sense eventually. I signed the drawing softly and titled it "Uncle Markus" before shutting the book.

"All right, time for your nap before we head over to Ivan's house," Mama said.

I nodded delicately, yawning. I was tired after all, and I wanted to be well rested when I confronted Uncle Markus. I was very smart. The doctors had said so, so I knew my deduction about him was correct. I just needed him to admit it, and then I would demand that he help my daddy now.

I let Mama lead me to my bed in the room we shared and tuck me in. She kissed my forehead gently and left me to rest. I yawned, snuggling down into the bed, holding the stuffed alligator Daddy had gotten me. Soon I was fast asleep, dreaming about flowers and butterflies and fangs.

*Lukai*

"*Puttana*, little mouse, I will find you and make you mine! Pain is all you will know!" I roared, pounding my fists on the soot-covered desk in Yuuta's incinerated room.

It had been the only thing that had survived the blaze, being made of solid metal. My ash-blackened hands shook as I raised them to my face, a mad laugh bursting from my chest as I trembled. I would kill his vampire in front of him, then chain him up for the rest of my life. He would know an eternity of loss and torture for this! No one leaves me. No one!

I stormed out of the room, kicking up ash in my wake, and it was fitting, as if the cloud of death followed me. It stuck to my skin, black as death. I *was* Death in human form. I would wreak havoc.

"Hey, Lukai, you have a mission—Urk!"

The other Hunter had stopped me in my tracks for such frivolity? I just slashed his throat and kept walking, feeling a laugh bubble up in my chest, the ash on my left hand swept away by crimson blood. I had bigger things to do, a higher calling. Nothing would stop me! Even if I had to paint my path in a swatch of bodies! The laughter escaped my chest as I approached the shattered window they had escaped through. It wouldn't stop! Kept spilling from me as I jumped out the window, my coat billowing around me, black against the stark day. I *am* Death! It was all they would know!

*Ivan*

Sitting at my desk, I let the two men sleep as I sketched away. I had woken with a sense of foreboding and couldn't get back to sleep. So now I poured over a sheet of card stock with a charcoal pencil and a heavy-duty eraser. I wasn't sure what I was sketching, but it wasn't something all light and pretty. In all honesty, it looked like I was drawing...*Death*, a haggard thin silhouette wearing a heavy black coat and carrying a sharp knife. The only thing I seemed inclined to give color to was the knife. It dripped with blood and seemed to be the focal point of the work. Why...did I draw this again? I rubbed my temples, getting a bit of a headache. Great, a vampire with a headache. Who'd ever heard of such a thing? I sighed, then jumped when arms wrapped around my shoulders suddenly. I was so preoccupied I hadn't heard anyone get up.

"You were the one who wanted more sleep, you little imp. Yet here you are, making the rest of us sleep while you are sitting up and...drawing? What's this all about?" Yuuta's voice murmured into my ear as he suddenly leaned forward and snatched the work off of the desk, still hanging over my shoulder.

His closeness made my heart race, his scent strong when he was this close. I was hungry, and he smelled so good.

"I don't know. I just felt like it, I suppose. I have a headache now though," I murmured, my mouth feeling dry as I spoke.

But it was the sudden rumble of my stomach that gave away my hunger.

"Hey, stupid, why didn't you say something? I can't help you if you keep it to yourself," he said, setting the drawing down and spinning my chair so I faced him.

"I'm new, so I'm always hungry," I muttered, blushing as he dropped to his knees so he was eye level with me in the chair.

"It's my job to ease that hunger, Ivan. It's why I'm here. Are you telling me you're going to start running from it? Like you told me Markus does? Don't be stupid," he said, pulling me close.

My heart clenched, and my frown formed deeply.

"You're here because I love you. The blood is just a plus," I muttered, blushing at the blatant admission.

I don't think I'd ever said it so easily in such a calm situation.

"I love you too, but you need me more for the blood than the love right now. I understand that. So stop being stubborn," he said, smiling a heartrendingly beautiful smile.

It made my heart ache and soar at the same time. It made me want to say yes to any and all of his requests. That was quite the disarming smile.

"All right. But promise me you know that I'm not just using you. I really do love you," I told him as he pulled me out of the chair and into his lap on the floor.

"I do know that. Otherwise, the smile wouldn't work," he said cheekily, kissing my cheek softly.

"Oh, that is dirty, mister," I said, nuzzling into his neck softly, feeling his laughter buzz against my lips as I kissed his skin.

"All is fair in love and war, little hot brand," he purred, then groaned lowly as I bit down on his pulse, my own groan following as his tangy blood splashed against my tongue.

We were quite the pair. That was for sure.

I drank eagerly from him, his arms snaking around my waist and pinning me tight against him. I groaned, feeling him grind his growing arousal against mine. I blushed deeply and shuddered, thinking that maybe this cycle of hunger and lust wasn't such a bad thing after all. We could manage it—and had been managing it—together so easily. I drew back from his neck with a gasp, shuddering as he ground against me again. My belly was full, but my lust was at an all-time high.

"You two seem to be having fun," I heard Markus purr from the bed and managed to get my wits about me enough to look over at him, blushing in embarrassment.

He was propped up on one arm, watching us with a smirk on his face.

"Feel free to join us, sinful Mark," Yuuta purred back, turning his head and grinning at Markus.

"Hmm…I think I'd rather watch this time," he replied, sitting up and stretching slowly.

I felt my blush deepen as I watched his muscles ripple with the movement.

"You're drooling, hot brand," Yuuta said bluntly.

"No, I'm not." I wiped my chin and flushed deeper still. "I am…," I muttered in embarrassment.

"Mm…don't be embarrassed, hot brand. It's a compliment. Right, sinful Mark?" Yuuta murmured with a grin, kissing me deeply.

I groaned and nipped delightedly at his lip.

"Most assuredly," Markus replied.

I heard him get up from the bed, approaching us. He pulled me up away from Yuuta's lips and leaned down. I thought he was going to kiss me, but instead his lips connected with Yuuta's. I gasped in soft surprise, then moaned lowly, watching them as they kissed in earnest as if they had done it before. I shuddered, feeling my cock twitch and jerk as I watched them, their tongues battling heatedly for dominance. It was the hottest thing I had ever seen. When they finally pulled back from each other, a strand of saliva connected between them.

"Holy fuck…" I groaned softly, biting my lip and grasping my cock, stroking slowly.

It was so hot watching them.

"Take good care of our Ivy, sweet flame," Markus said to him as he drew away, caressing his face gently.

"I will. Gotta get this lust stamped down before our guests arrive," Yuuta murmured, smirking as he reached out and wrapped his hand around mine on my cock, his eyes still locked with Markus's.

"That's the plan. I should be back in time to help out, but if not, be sure to wear him out," Markus said with a grin before standing lithely and going to dress.

"As you wish," Yuuta purred, forcing my hands to stroke faster.

I moaned lowly, my head falling back in delight, nearly whacking it on the edge of the desk. "Mm…that's it, little hot brand. Shut off your mind and just feel," he growled, gently shoving me to the side with his free hand so I fell flat and would no longer risk braining myself on the desk with every reaction. Thank God for plush carpets.

I opened my mouth to respond but only sputters came out as my mind went blank, the wet heat of Yuuta's mouth engulfing my cock suddenly without the slightest warning. My hips bucked instinctively, craving more of that delicious heat. He didn't protest or pin my hips, just reached a hand up to massage my balls while his tongue worked my aching shaft. Shudders racked my form as the tip of my cock leaked from the stimulation.

"Ah! Yuuta…" I moaned wantonly, lacing my fingers in his hair, freeing it from the ponytail that had contained it.

His response was to suck hard as he started to move his head, his hands squeezing my balls lightly. My hips bucked again, and he just went with it, a groan vibrating around my throbbing length when I hit the back of his throat.

"So g-good! More…more…" I panted, shuddering again as he rose up a bit.

A hand tapped my hip as his eyes met with mine. Thrust, he wanted me to thrust into his mouth. So I did, moaning as it sent sparks of pleasure through my overheated body. His tongue flicked around the shaft of my cock, agile as I thrust haphazardly between his lips, lewd sounds spilling from my mouth like a sieve.

I came in a sudden hot rush that took my mind with it, leaving me a moaning mess as he quickly gulped down all I had to offer. I blushed deeply, realizing he had gotten good at being able to tell when I was close. He'd been ready for it. He drew up off of me, kissing the tip gently. It made me cry out, oversensitive after such a powerful release.

"Mm…delicious as ever, hot brand. How are you feeling?" he purred teasingly, crawling slowly until his body hung over mine, the tip of his cock brushing against my thigh.

I bit my lip, lust surging up in me again despite having already come.

"Great. I want more. I want you inside of me again," I said unabashedly.

I felt my mojo coming back. I missed being so suave. I was back in business, baby. He blinked and grinned.

"Exactly what I wanted to hear, hot brand," he purred, standing and yanking me up to my feet.

I had been so distracted I didn't know when Markus had left, which had probably made him a smirking madman on the way out. I'd get him back for it later when he was least expecting it.

Yuuta shoved me backward onto the bed, and I let myself fall onto it, sprawled out openly with my legs parted and my knees bent over the edge of the bed. He stood between them, looking down at me with an expression of lust and admiration. I blushed deeply and felt the strangest urge to cover myself as if I had any form of modesty.

"Stop staring. I need you..." I whimpered, squirming against the covers.

He smirked, placing a hand in the middle of my chest and stroking along my skin, raising goosebumps. He smiled in delight and grabbed the bottle of lube up off the nightstand.

"That look on your face is beautiful, little one," he purred softly, slickening up a couple of fingers before lifting one of my legs and pressing one into the puckered ring of my asshole.

I groaned lowly, blushing fiercely as he did so, curling the digit inside me with no warning.

"You're...a fucking...tease..." I panted, squirming as he added a second finger and started to thrust them slowly.

It forced moans from my lips as he pinned my hip with one hand to the bed, his other still thrusting his fingers inside of me. A jolt ran through me as he curled his fingers and hit that spot inside of me, making me cry out.

"Stop complaining. We both know you love it," he purred, scissoring his fingers sharply against the spot, making my body arch off the bed.

I shuddered, moaning as he continued to torture me, stroking that spot mercilessly.

"Ah-ha! Please…I need you…" I whimpered, clutching at the sheets and thrashing as he hit that spot again.

He chuckled and withdrew his fingers from me, leaving me feeling empty.

"I love the sound of desperation in your voice, little hot brand," he purred, lifting my other leg so both of my legs rested on his shoulders.

Clutching my hip with one hand, he used the other to spread more lube on his cock before guiding it to my asshole, rubbing the head teasingly against it. I let out a sound of frustration, bucking my hips at the right moment to impale myself on him, grinning in satisfaction when his moan echoed mine. I slid my heels off his shoulders and locked my legs around his waist so he couldn't try and tease me more. I shuddered and gasped as he suddenly slammed to the hilt into me. It was a rough action, rougher than usual, and he froze, looking down at me with concern. But it hadn't hurt me, not even slightly. My body was stronger now, more durable. I smiled, leaning up and kissing him deeply.

"Do it again. Use all that strength of yours. I won't break," I whispered against his lips, nipping his tongue before letting myself fall back against the sheets.

He swallowed, blushing nervously. But he nodded and grabbed my hips with both hands, thrusting hard into me again. I cried out as it sent sparks of pleasure through my body. I grabbed his arms and held on as he began to pound into me mercilessly. The pleasure began to come with an edge of pain, but the feel was so mixed it only brought moans of delight from my lips.

"Ah…hot brand, I don't think…I can hold out much longer. Are you close?" Yuuta groaned, gritting his teeth as he thrust hard and to the hilt into me, the pleasure seeming to reverberate through my body coated with that tantalizing edge of pain.

"Yes! God, more of that, Yuuta! Please!" I moaned, my legs tightening around his waist as his thrusts sped up.

My vision went white, and I screamed out as my climax hit me like a freight train, my cum shooting hotly across my chest. Yuuta cried out as my body clenched and spasmed around him, thrusting as deep as he could before he came heavily. He collapsed forward, barely catching himself on his arms over me, panting softly as his hair fell around our faces like a blackened waterfall.

"That…was intense. Ivan, I love you. Dear God, do I love you," he said, his voice gruff and breathy.

"I love you too, forever and always, my beloved Hunter," I said, feeling my heart swell with the love it was filled with.

He smiled and shakily sat up, pulling out of me, then frowned, looking down at where we had been merged.

"Are you sure I didn't hurt you? There's blood…," he said, concerned.

I blinked softly and sat up, feeling a little bit of a twinge but nothing horribly discomforting. I looked down and saw that there was a thin coating of blood on his cock and a few trickles out of my asshole but nothing that horrible. I'd seen worse in bad pornos.

"I'm fine, just a few twinges, but you can't have mind-blowing sex and not feel it afterward. It'd be a different story if I couldn't walk while we have company coming over shortly," I said, smiling easily to reassure him.

He swallowed, blushing brightly. The door cracked open slowly, and Markus eased into the room, blinking at the scene before him. He looked at the look on Yuuta's face, my reassuring smile, and the blood between us and burst out laughing.

"Trying out Ivan's new durability, I see. Come on. Let's shower and get cleaned up. Miriam and Danny will be here in a few hours. I bought all of us some nice outfits for tonight since we'll be introducing Zarrack and Yuuta to them tonight," Markus said, holding up a couple of shopping bags.

"Thank you, Marky. Come on. Let's get cleaned up. We made quite the mess," I said, sitting up and pushing Yuuta toward the bathroom as Markus set the bags on the vanity and followed us into the bathroom.

I smiled as I remembered Yuuta's reaction to the luxury bathroom last night. I had the large bathtub and the wonderful walk-in shower with three showerheads installed not long after I'd moved into the master bedroom. Both were big enough to fit two or three people, and it was perfect for when I wanted a spa day of sorts.

Markus started the taps in the shower, making sure the temperature was right, before stripping off his clothing, smiling as I pushed Yuuta into the spray. He still looked so unsure, but I really was okay. Markus beat me to the point as he joined us in the shower and pulled the glass door shut.

"Yuuta, it looked to me like you two had had the best, mind-blowing sex in the world. Don't ruin it with unnecessary worrying. He really is more durable, and Ivan would tell you if you'd hurt him. He's very straightforward, especially when it comes to pain. So cheer up, would you?" Markus purred, caging Yuuta against the shower wall.

I blushed, finding I like the scene very much. But I tamped it down, trying to control the wild lust that kept surging up inside me. We didn't have time for another round. That was for sure.

"You're right. I'm sorry," Yuuta murmured softly, smiling and placing a chaste kiss on Markus's lips.

Markus smiled, stroking Yuuta's long hair gently.

"Good. Now let's get cleaned up and dressed. Miriam texted me and said she had something to tell us and that she wanted us to 'keep an open mind and not hate her.' I don't know what she means by that, but it sounded ominous," he said softly, his brow furrowing as he thought about it.

I rolled my eyes and smiled.

"Probably something trivial. She gets worked up over the smallest things," I said and wet my hair.

We would find out now, wouldn't we? I wasn't worried.

# Chapter 12

# Family and Blood

*Ivan*

I sat at the vanity, blushing in embarrassment as my hair was being used to teach Yuuta how to braid. Markus was carefully teaching him the technique for the easiest braid he knew. I flinched when the braid was finished and pulled tight.

"Hey, gentle back there!" I exclaimed, looking at my own pouty face in the mirror.

Though I had to admit, it was pretty good for his first attempt at braiding.

"This is why I just put mine back into a ponytail or have Ivan braid it for me, because his braids are always so perfect and pretty," he said, purring the compliment at me.

"Fine, he can do it for you. But you really should learn how to do it. Your hair is just so long a ponytail is not enough to contain it," Markus said, pouting himself now.

I laughed softly and patted the floor in front of me.

"All right, Yuuta, sit. I'll braid it for you," I said, smiling as he eagerly plopped down in front of me.

I ran a comb carefully through his long, thick onyx-colored hair, plaiting it with deft fingers. It was so much easier and slicker looking now that I was more agile, making a nice, tight braid that wouldn't come apart before the night was over.

"There. Beautiful," I murmured, leaning down and kissing his shoulder lovingly.

He stood up and smiled.

"Thank you, little one. I'll get dressed now. You two are making me feel underdressed," he said jokingly, gesturing to the fact that Markus and I had already donned the slacks Markus had bought for us.

"All right, I'll get the rest of my clothes on and do my makeup," I murmured softly, reaching for the lovely gray button-up Markus had picked out for me.

I slid it on and carefully buttoned the buttons, tucking the bottom into the slacks. The matching bow tie came next, the gray slightly darker than the button-up but not so dark as to look black like the slacks. I expertly tied the bow tie into place and straightened it, simple. A frustrated sound came from Yuuta, who—I could see in the mirror—was clearly struggling with the bow tie. Markus sighed playfully and went to help him. He'd chosen a red button-up for Yuuta with a black, gray, and red bowtie. The colors were really perfect for him, just as the colors Markus had chosen for me and himself were perfect. Markus had an eye for fashion that was even better than mine, and that was scary. Markus was already dressed in his deep-forest-green button-up and a softer green and black-colored bow tie. He tied the bow around Yuuta's neck gently and kissed his cheek before drawing back. I smiled happily and reached for the eyeliner that sat atop my vanity. I carefully rimmed my eyes with black and used a smoky eyeshadow that made my eyes look like a foggy forest. Then I used a pale-pink lipstick with a gray lip liner. I happily surveyed the results in the mirror, happy that it came out perfect, making my eyes seem stark and wild. Makeup was like magic in my opinion.

"Beautiful as always, Ivy. You look like an avenging fallen angel," Markus murmured softly, kissing my cheek gently.

The doorbell dinged, and I smiled, standing up.

"They're here. I'll get the door. You go into the living room and behave," I said, darting out the door, adoring this speed of mine as I made it down to the door before Zarrack had even left the kitchen.

"I could have gotten it," he muttered, wiping his hands off on his apron, or rather my apron he'd found in the kitchen supply closet.

"She doesn't know you yet, so I got it," I said, getting to the door and opening it.

Miriam stood on the front mat, holding Danny's hand and a bottle of wine. I frowned at her, mad that she had spent her own hard-earned money on something I had stocked in the basement.

"Hey, honey, how much did that cost?" I asked, digging my wallet out of my pocket.

I would give her the money back. She needn't spend her meager funds on us when I have enough for everyone and then some.

"You know I'm not going to tell you. It's fine, really. The wine is warranted, especially after what I need to tell you," she said, brushing past me and toward the kitchen.

"Wait!" I called to stop her before she ran into Zarrack. "I have a couple people I want you to meet. They've become a part of this ragtag family of mine, and I'd love for you to meet them," I said softly, glad when she stopped moving for me.

"Oh, all right. Are they coming over?" she asked, heading into the kitchen.

"We're already here, actually, miss," Zarrack said, making Miriam squeak and drop the bottle of wine.

I automatically moved to catch it and was actually fast enough to get it before it smashed on the floor, blinking as I hoped Miriam hadn't actually seen me move in her startled state.

But then my eyes met with Danny's. Shock was written on his little face. He had seen it, seen my inhuman speed. I stood up and handed the bottle to Zarrack, biting back my panic.

"Zarrack, could you put this on ice and meet us in the living room? It would seem we all have much to discuss," I said softly, ushering the two toward the living room.

Zarrack had seen that Danny had seen my actions, conveying his concerns through his eyes.

In the living room, Miriam stood, blinking at the two sitting on the couch who were currently engaged in a passionate kiss. I just groaned, rubbing at the stress headache forming between my eyelids. Could this be going any worse?

"Miriam, this is Yuuta. He is our...boyfriend," I said, clearing my throat to get the two to separate as Zarrack came into the room and sat carefully in the armchair. "And this is Zarrack, our best friend. He's become like a brother to me, so be nice," I said softly, trying to lighten the tense atmosphere.

"It's...nice to meet you, Yuuta, Zarrack. I have no right to judge you on your new friends, Ivan, because...I have been keeping a secret from you for ten years now...and it was wrong of me. You should have known from the very beginning," she said, gripping the hem of her shirt as she seemed to struggle with the weight of whatever it was she wanted to confess.

"What is it, Miriam? Surely it's nothing so horrible that I wouldn't forgive you for keeping it from me. You had to have your reasons," I said, touching her shoulder reassuringly as I gently eased her onto the couch beside Markus.

"No, Ivan. Danny...he's your son, okay? I didn't tell you because I was afraid you'd hate me. So I kept it a secret from you. You were only experimenting back then, just discovering your sexuality. I knew how you would take it. I knew you would want to do the honorable thing and marry me. But I couldn't let you throw your life away on a mistake. Danny was a miracle, but you being his father was a mistake. Telling you the truth would have ruined your life. You would never have met Markus...or this Yuuta fellow...if I had been so selfish. So I lied and let you be everything to Danny except his father. But then you almost died, and...and I couldn't lie anymore. I couldn't let you go to the grave without knowing that the little boy you loved so much was *yours*. I just couldn't!" she exclaimed, tears rolling down her cheeks heavily.

The air left my lungs all at once, shock shuddering through me as I turned to look at the little boy, who smiled brightly at me. He'd known it all along. Of that, I had no doubt. My son, he was my baby boy. I already loved him dearly. I could love him as his father without missing a beat. *I had a son.*

"Danny is my son…my baby boy…Did you hear that, Markus?" I asked, tears rolling down my cheeks as the love in my heart overflowed again.

I didn't even stop to think that my tears would no longer be clear. Curse my emotional self.

"That's wonderful, Ivy. Why don't you sit down? You look like you're going to faint," Markus said, getting up and easing me down onto the seat.

Danny came over and climbed into my lap, looking up at Markus.

"Thank you for saving my daddy, Uncle Markus. Thank you so much," he said, smiling brightly and poking at my lips. "Can I see them?" he asked.

My heart dropped.

"Wh-what do you mean, buddy? See what?" I asked.

He knew that Markus was a vampire, that he'd saved me by making me one. But how?

"Children are so observant," Zarrack said with a smile and a laugh, "you may as well come out with it. You're as good as outed already," he added, smiling good-naturedly and sweeping up a blood-pinkened tear from my cheek.

"What do you mean? Come out with what?" Miriam asked gently, frowning softly at me.

"One more secret to reveal and I promise no more secrets between us," I said, rubbing the back of my neck, feeling exhausted. "Markus and I are vampires. Markus has been one since before we'd met. He just turned me in order to save my life," I said slowly, looking at her as I held Danny close, baring my fangs at him so he could see them.

"Wow, Daddy! They're so cool!" he exclaimed, reaching up gently and poked at one.

I caught his wrist carefully.

"Careful, Danny. They're very sharp," I said, smiling at him gently.

He smiled back and leaned into me, hugging me tightly.

"I love you, Daddy. I'm so glad you're safe. I'm glad you know now so I can call you daddy instead of uncle," Danny said, snuggling up to me.

"I know, buddy. But now everything can go back to normal, just with less secrets. I will most assuredly be moving you and your mother into this house. You are my son and my family. You will be treated as such," I said, smiling at Danny and Miriam.

"That is unnecessary…really," Miriam said, frowning deeply.

I frowned in response, cuddling my beloved son.

"I definitely wanna live here! I can see Daddy and Uncle Markus and Mr. Yuuta and Mr. Zarrack every day! We can play games, and Dad can help me with my homework. Please, Mommy! Please, can we move in!" Danny exclaimed, leaping into her lap.

My little energetic monkey, just like I was at that age.

"Well…all right…but not because we can't afford to live on our own," she said, holding Danny gently.

"I know that, Miriam. But I want to have you and my son close. I've gone through the worst ordeals recently, and all I really want is to have my family nearby, especially now that I know that this boy I already adored so much is really my son. There is so much I want to teach him so he can grow up to be just as smart and creative as his mother and father. Did you know your mommy was an art major in college? She paints the most beautiful flowers," I said gently, still unable to truly grasp just how lucky I was.

"All right…I'll do it then, for Danny's sake, because he loves you so much and has wanted to spend more time with you than he's been able to," she replied, smiling softly and blushing in embarrassment at my comments, no doubt.

"Good. You don't have to right away. Get things settled, and I'll be waiting to help move you in," I said and smiled.

"Dinner is ready," Zarrack murmured, poking his head in the living room doorway.

"Well then, let's eat. We'll have to use the dining room. I don't usually entertain this many guests," I said but stood and led everyone into the underused, dusty dining room.

"Er…perhaps we should dine on the patio?" Markus said, wiping his finger through the thick layer of dust on the table and quirking an eyebrow at Zarrack and me.

"Don't look at me. The cook doesn't set the table!" Zarrack exclaimed, looking frazzled in his stained apron.

Danny burst out into haphazard giggles, and I couldn't help but smile. No one said we were perfect, but we were family. So back patio dinner it was, and what a wonderful dinner it was, perhaps the last one for a long time.

*Yuuta*

I sat washing the dishes while Ivan dried and put them away. It had been a long night, and I couldn't be prouder of him. He had controlled the fledgling hunger even as Danny had clung to him and poked at his fangs. The little boy had spent the majority of the visit in his arms for Lord's sake, and he hadn't broken and bitten the boy. I had always thought that vampires couldn't control their urges, let alone with the blood of the young. Zarrack was right that the two vampires were far from the evil ones we had come to know and despise.

"Ugh, I'm so tired," Markus groaned, putting the last of the leftovers into the fridge.

I laughed softly, smiling.

"Says the one who hardly did anything at all," I teased, getting a smack on the ass. "Hey!" I exclaimed, glaring at him over my shoulder.

"You have to admit you deserved that one," Ivan said from beside me, giggling.

Suddenly Markus's arms engulfed us both, and his face rested on my shoulder.

"I love you, my beloveds," he murmured softly, his deep voice rumbling against my ear.

I blushed softly as Ivan leaned his head against us both and smiled up at us.

"I love you too. I think tonight I just want to be held. After everything that's transpired, I really just want to lie with my lovers and just simply live. No more death or destruction. Just our happy couple and nothing more," Ivan said, nuzzling against my arm as he dried the last dish.

"I agree with that. And I love you both very much. Both of you need to feed tonight, and then we can just rest. Tomorrow is a new day with nothing planned. Let's just live normally for once, as normal as a Hunter and two vampires can," I said, leaning into the warmth of my two lovers.

They were wonderful and beautiful, and having them be part of my life made me happier than I had ever been.

"Yuuta, you don't have to feed me. Your main focus is Ivan. I'm far from a fledgling, so I can go several days without blood," Markus murmured, drawing back as I leaned forward to drain the sink.

"I want to. You may be able to, but you don't have to. As a Hunter, my body can take it. I want to feed you both and to lie with you both. This is the path I have willingly chosen. To show that I love you and will never despise you, I will give you the blood in my veins because I know you would never abuse such a gift. Neither of you would," I said, turning and looking up at him with a fierce expression.

He looked startled but leaned down and kissed me gently, his lips soft and loving.

"Come on. Let's go to bed," Ivan murmured, taking our hands and pulling us up the stairs.

The little hot brand was always so perfect, his actions making me smile. I could truly be happy with him—them. Markus and Ivan had simply accepted me and drew me as part of their happy family despite all I had done and despite what I was. I felt the happiness surge up in me in the form of tears, spilling over and making Ivan pause in the doorway to the bedroom.

"What's wrong?" Markus asked, beating him to the punch, both concerned.

I couldn't help it. I laughed in delight and wrapped my arms around them both.

"Nothing. For once, everything is right in the world," I said, beaming happily.

Markus smiled, kissing away my tears with gentle lips.

"Come. The day is over, and it's time to rest. We can rejoice in the morning," he said, keeping his smile as I reluctantly released him.

He was right. It was late, and we were all tired from the events that had befallen us this night. We replaced the nice clothes with pajamas and curled up together beneath the sheets, a moment of simplicity amidst the insanity of our lives.

I wrapped my arms around their shoulders and pulled them close. No words were needed between us as they easily buried their faces into either side of my neck. Even the ecstasy of the bite seemed calmer, relaxed, as we finally just held each other. It was as if one chapter had ended but another more beautiful one had begun. It was still written in blood and tarnished by despair and pain, but the beauty eased the burden, if only a little bit.

# Chapter 13

# Darkness Comes

*Lukai*

It had taken a lot of work, but I located them. Ivan hid himself away from the world of his own accord, long before he'd become a part of this twisted realm. Smart boy, it would take the authorities a long time to find us and the hell I would put them through.

I approached the back of the house, hearing the sounds of laughter from inside. I had waited until young Zarrack had gone. I had no score with him, so I would let him live unless he interfered. I quietly opened the door, hearing movement approaching me. I lifted my dagger, planning to plant it in the gut of whoever it was.

*Ivan*

"I'll be right back. I need some fresh air," Yuuta said, smiling as he stood up from his chair at the kitchen table.

We sat together, eating breakfast and talking. It felt so natural, like we'd been doing it forever. I smiled at him and pulled him down for a soft kiss.

"Hurry back. Or we'll have to drag you back," Markus said, lifting a glass of orange juice to his lips.

Yuuta laughed at his words, stealing his glass and taking a swig.

"You got it, sinful Mark," he purred, returning his glass to him and walking away sassily.

I laughed happily, leaning into Markus.

"I am so happy, Marky. I could live like this forever," I said softly, smiling gently.

The dream was shattered so suddenly when Yuuta cried out and all I could smell was blood.

"Yuuta!" I cried as Markus and I rushed after him, terrified for our human love.

The scene we were greeted with was horrendous, making me stumble back with a horrified, shocked scream. Yuuta was on the floor, leaned against the wall as he held his stomach, a large blade sticking out of him as Lukai stood over him, sneering.

"Not so strong now, are we?" Lukai hissed, kicking him hard in the side.

Yuuta cried out, blood pooling around him on the floor. Markus let out a growl and leapt at the Hunter, the two clashing against the back door, making the house shake as it broke outward and sent them flying into the backyard. I kept looking back and forth between them and Yuuta, panicking. What was I supposed to do? Who was I supposed to help? Who needed me more? Was I going to lose Yuuta? So soon? Now I sounded like Markus. But he was a Hunter. He wouldn't want to become a vampire even at the cost of his life, would he?

"Stop...looking so panicked. Go help him. He came first," Yuuta said, looking so pale and broken, the pool of crimson on the floor deepening. "Kill that bastard for me, won't you? It won't make you a monster...You're simply defending your territory. Never not protect yourself, hot brand," Yuuta said, breathing labored as he held the knife in place.

"Don't...talk like that...You're not gonna die...You hear me? Don't act like you won't still be here to protect me...," I said, feeling the tears on my face.

But I didn't care. He gave a pained laugh, trembling as he reached out to caress my cheek with a bloodied hand. The blood mingled with my bloodied tears, a macabre union between us.

"You're so silly. A strong man like you…never needed a protector…," he said, his voice trailing off as his hand fell away from my face and his breathing subsided.

"Y-Yuuta? Yuuta! No! Come back to me. You can't leave me, you bastard!" I cried, shaking him.

His head just lolled limply to the side, his body slack and his eyes half closed.

"Yuuta!" I yowled and felt a rage I had never possessed before surge up inside me.

I gently laid Yuuta on his back and slowly pulled the blade out of him, fighting the urge to gag as I wiped his blood off on my pants. There came a stilling inside me, and my eyes went cold, my hand tightening on the handle of the blade. Lukai had signed his death warrant in Yuuta's blood, and I wasn't going to stop until the bastard breathed his last breath.

# Epilogue

*Yuuta*

I could feel the blood in my lungs and could feel it spilling out of me as I died. Death was inevitable for a mortal like myself, but I had never thought it would come like this so soon. The pain of it was nothing compared to the loss I was feeling as Ivan sobbed down at me, begging me not to go. Even as my consciousness slipped away, I could still hear him, at least for a little while before all went dark and silent. I wish I knew how to describe it, but part of me wouldn't wish such truth upon anyone. I could only hope that Markus would be able to comfort Ivan now that I was gone. I knew they could defeat Lukai together. They were my everything. I let myself fall into the darkness of death, embracing my end, knowing I had spent my last days happier than I had ever been.

*Markus*

"I just have to kill you, and Ivan will be all mi-ine," Lukai's singsongy voice echoed through the trees around me.

For once, I cursed Ivan's choice to live out in the middle of nowhere. The trees gave the psychotic Hunter the perfect cover to hide, the rot of nature hiding and scattering his scent.

"How can you just kill one of your own like it was nothing? Yuuta was a Hunter just like you!" I shouted, grasping a hold of my rage, using it to fuel my senses as I tried to find the tainted bastard amidst the trees.

"Traitor. Not that I care. They're all fodder for the machine, the war. When one falls, more crops up in its place. Hehe. It's time we destroy you people once and for all."

His voice most assuredly came from my left this time. The animals had gone silent as if they sensed the coming battle and had gone into hiding. They were right as I turned on my heel and launched toward a shadow I could now make out as the Hunter. But the bastard evaded my attack, swinging up onto the branch above me with a taunting laugh. I hissed in pain as something whistled past my face, cutting my cheek. My eyes followed the sound, finding an arrow buried in the tree behind me.

"Fucking pussy! Get down here and fight me like a man!" I snarled as I looked up to find him leaping across to another tree.

"Why should I fight like a man when you are no man at all?" he asked, holding up a hand crossbow and aiming at me again.

I was prepared this time, dodging out of the way and launching up onto the branch beneath him.

"Besides, it's so much easier this way," he exclaimed, suddenly appearing on the branch next to me.

Before I could think, he was pulling the trigger on the crossbow.

CPSIA information can be obtained
at www.ICGtesting.com
Printed in the USA
BVHW051057310722
643467BV00010B/46

9 781638 819660